SURVIVING BEAR ISLAND

BY

PAUL GRECI

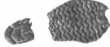

MOVE BOOKS

NOTE FROM THE PUBLISHER

*The Move Books team is committed to
inspiring readers everywhere.*

Text copyright © 2015 by Paul Greci
Illustration copyright © by James Madsen
Book design by Virginia Pope

First paperback edition, November 2017
First published in hardcover in March 2015 by Move Books

Library of Congress Control Number: 2014960255
ISBN: 978-0-692-97736-1

10 9 8 7 6 5 4 3 2 1
Printed in the U.S.A.

MOVING BOYS TO READ

P.O. Box 183
Beacon Falls, Connecticut, 06403

To my parents, Joseph and Dolores Greci,
for encouraging the adventurer in me.
— *Paul Greci*

To my parents who brought me up
in the outdoors.
— *Jim Madsen*

MAP OF BEAR ISLAND

Orca
Mountain

Shallow Bay

Bear
Peak

Goose
Tongue
Cove

Silver
Camp

Eagle Ridge

Coho Bay

The
Sentinels

Whale Bay

Dana
Point

Otter
Cove

Cook's
Cove

CHAPTER 1

A WALL of dog-like heads was closing in on us. Sea lions, six or eight of them, swam side by side. They raced toward us like they were gonna swim right through us, stretching their necks and plowing through the water like they had motors attached to their backs. I gripped my paddle tighter and held it just above the water, waiting, watching, just like Dad. Then, at the last second, they dove.

"They could've dumped us if they wanted to," Dad said. "It's happened to other kayakers."

I felt some bumps right under my feet, and the nose of the kayak shifted.

"Crazy," I said. "You feel that?" The last thing I wanted was to take a swim. We'd be in trouble if we dumped. The water would freeze us solid.

"Never been touched like that," Dad said. "Let's paddle. Now."

I dipped my kayak paddle into the blue-green salt water and pulled. Then did it again. And again. I twisted side to side, pulling one blade through the water while pushing the other through the air. Like Dad always said, "You get your back muscles working for you when you paddle. If you just relied on your arms you'd be trashed in a couple hours."

Left.

Right.

Left.

Right.

Sea lions swam along on both sides of the kayak, easily matching our pace.

Just as I pushed my paddle in again, a gust of wind came out of nowhere and water slammed into my face, running down and underneath my raincoat. I felt the sweat building under my raincoat and rain pants and just wanted to crawl out of them. At the same time my hands were turning to ice from being washed by the waves and chilled by the wind.

The sea lions dove under the boat, nudging it. Two of them surfaced right next to me, and opened their mouths and made these roaring sounds that made my breath catch. Then they dove again and disappeared.

I couldn't see Dad, but I knew he was behind me, using the rudder to steer, keeping us pointed at an angle to the foot-high waves to help steady the kayak. Left. Right. Left. Right. I was a first-time kayaker.

Left. Right. Dad was the expert.

Left. Right. More water stinging my face.

Left. Rubbery arms.

Right. More water up my sleeves.

Left. I can't feel my hands.

Right. Where are those sea lions?

Left. This was so Mom and Dad's thing. I just agreed to go because this was the first time in three years that my dad actually acted like he wanted to do something with me.

I tried to keep paddling, but the water was dragging my arms down.

My body was burning but my face was freezing in place and my hands were completely numb. And to make matters worse, the gray clouds looked like they would dump on us any moment. But hey, that's how it is in Prince William Sound, Alaska. You come out here to kayak, your muscles work overtime, and you expect rain. We'd been gone for two and a half weeks and still had sixty miles to paddle to get to Whittier and then a four hundred mile drive north to Fairbanks. I just wanted to get home.

The kayak slowed down. I stopped paddling and twisted my body around.

"Just making a clothing adjustment so I don't overheat," Dad said. His paddle was lying across his cockpit as he wrestled with his raincoat and life vest. "Looks pretty rocky ahead, but I'm gonna try to work us closer to shore. Hopefully that's the last we've seen of those sea lions."

I nodded, turned back around and waited. Mom should've been with us. Everything was better when Mom was around.

I scanned the water. No sign of the sea lions. And the waves seemed to be calming down. Little did I know I would be upside down in the water in less than an hour—fighting for my life.

CHAPTER 2

I BROKE the surface and spit salt water.

Shore. Shore. Shore, my mind screamed.

But my dad. My dad. Where was he?

I yanked my hood off and stretched my neck. Giant green waves tipped with white surrounded me. I jumped and twisted.

"Dad!" I yelled. No orange anywhere.

Another wave slapped my face and I spit more salt water. I grabbed at a slippery log but another wave ripped it from my grip.

Then I angled toward shore. Alone. I kicked and kicked, but my rubber boots were filled with water and dragged me down. And the cold slashed me from all directions, like a sharp knife. My life vest was riding up on my neck, driving my head down. The waves washed over me from behind and kept dunking my head. I kept crawling forward with my arms trying to swim.

But my legs wouldn't rise. I felt like ropes were attached to my feet and I was being reeled down.

Down.

Down.

Down.

My head went under again and I pulled harder with my arms but they were moving in slow motion. My lungs burned for air.

I kept reaching and kicking—trying to get my mouth above the surface.

Don't take a breath, I thought. Don't.

My lips touched the air, but another wave broke on the back of my head, pushed me under and forward, and I inhaled salt water.

My feet bumped the bottom, sending a jolt through my spine. I pushed upward, felt the wind on my cheeks and coughed up the water. I sucked air and my chest burned like a forest fire. Then I saw the biggest wave -

It body-surfed me up the beach, filling my mouth and scrubbing my ears with a salt-watery grit.

The waves kept rolling in. Stacking on top of each other. Too many for me to keep track of. I just kept pulling with my arms and pushing with my legs, trying to keep from scraping the bottom, breathing when I could get my mouth above the surface.

The water sucked back, and for a moment, I was free. Just lying on the rocky beach. I pushed with my arms and legs, kneeling on all fours, then a wave poured over my back like cement from a mixer, and drove me up the beach. I tried to stand and get away from the water, but the retreating surf tackled me at the knees and yanked me back toward the water.

Crawl, I told myself. Get yourself above the strand line. I had to get beyond that strip of nasty seaweed along the beach.

Water hissed around my knees, covered my hands, and tried to pull me back toward the disaster behind me.

I forced my numb arms and legs forward, pushed through the slimy seaweed in the strand line and collapsed onto my stomach, with my head just under the towering evergreens. The next wave tugged at my feet, so I clawed my way farther into the forest.

I flipped onto my back, pulled my knees to my chest, and breathed.

Yeah, I'd made it to shore. But what about Dad? I gagged, then rolled onto my side. The salt-watery puke burned my throat.

I rose to my knees and wiped my mouth with the back of my hand, which covered my lips with spruce and hemlock needles. I spit and tried to blow the needles off my lips, then wiped my mouth again.

I pulled myself up and stepped out of the forest. Both my knees ached like the caps had been struck with a hammer. Big drops of cold rain pelted my face. I placed my hand just above my eyes and searched the white-capped waves for the orange of my dad's life preserver.

"Da-a-d," I tried to yell. "Da-a-d." My voice sounded strange. It was stretched out and slow, like a sheep baaaing. I rubbed my face with my hands, then cupped them over my mouth and breathed, and kept working on my cheeks until they could move on their own.

"Dad!"

Dad!

Dad!

Dad!

But all I heard was the boom of the waves as they broke on the beach, and a hiss as they were sucked back into the sea. And the wind flapping my hood.

I ran north along the rocky beach, my feet sloshing in my boots, my kneecaps stinging with every step. I kept ducking into the forest, hoping Dad had washed up and crawled under the trees like I had.

I called out again and again, and kept calling until my voice gave out. At the base of a rocky point where a small stream carved its way toward the sea, I dropped to my knees and pounded the beach with my fists. I rolled onto my side, then curled into a ball.

Where was he?

Dad. Dad. Dad, my mind screamed.

The rain pounded my exposed side—big, fat drops making dull thuds on my raingear, like the clouds were dropping marbles on me. I knew if I just lay here, I'd be dead soon. But I didn't want to move. Didn't want to face whatever there was to face, alone.

I rolled onto my stomach, pushed with my arms and stood up. I scanned the water again.

Monstrous green waves, topped with white froth, ran to the horizon.

My head fell forward and my chin pressed into my life vest.

This was my fault. All my fault. My mistake. My stupid mistake. I kicked the beach and sent small stones tumbling toward the surf.

A massive shiver took control of my body and for several seconds wouldn't let go. The wind was gonna freeze me solid if I didn't take shelter.

My hand brushed my side and I felt the bump in my jacket pocket, the survival kit Dad insisted I carry. I hadn't touched it since I stuffed it into my pocket at the start of the trip—August first—almost three weeks ago.

I turned my back on the water, and the wind pushed me into the forest. On the back side of a massive spruce as wide as a dump truck, I worked the kit out of my pocket.

Tom. Tom. Listen.

"Dad," I said. "Dad?"

I walked all the way around the tree but saw nothing.

You never know, son, but in case something happens and you get into a pinch, it doesn't hurt to be prepared. It's unlikely, but in case we find ourselves separated from each other or from our gear, at least you'll have something.

I turned in a circle, searching. "Dad?" I called again. "Dad?" But saw nothing but green. Wet green.

But his voice, I'd heard it. And, he'd said those exact words when he'd handed me the kit.

Dad had made it himself, double-bagged in one-gallon Ziploc baggies. The kit was bulky, always causing my pocket to catch on the combing of the cockpit when I got in and out of the kayak. I hated it. I wanted to put it somewhere else, but Dad had said, "No. Absolutely not."

"Whatever," I'd said, as I stuffed the monster into my pocket. "Like I'm really gonna need it."

"I hope you don't. But if you do, you'll have it."

And now, holding it in my hands, the kit felt small. Incredibly small.

I knelt gently on the back side of the tree, and checked it out:

> 1 emergency blanket
>
> 1 lighter
>
> 1 small box waterproof matches
>
> 2 pixie fishing lures with treble hooks
>
> 1 bunch of fishing line
>
> 1 pocket knife about four inches long
>
> 2 Meal Pack bars
>
> 6 small pieces of rope
>
> 1 small piece of flint
>
> 4 two-inch-long fire starter sticks

I leaned forward. Moisture from my nose dripped onto the knife.

My teeth knocked together like one of those wind-up chattering-teeth toys. I stood, and jumped up and down, rubbed my hands together, then stuffed everything back into the bags to keep it all dry.

Without a fire, I was as good as dead.

Look for dead tree branches that are attached to big trees. They stay the driest during the rain.

Where was he? Just in my head? Those words, his words, his voice, echoed in my mind. It sounded like he was right next to me. I glanced around again, but saw nothing.

I worked in a fury, snapping dead branches from big trees, and then piled them on the backside of the spruce. I knelt, and scraped away a layer of wet needles. With the lighter, I lit a fire starter stick, fed it dry twigs, and got a small fire going.

I held my hands—white and wrinkled—over the pocket-sized flames, hungry for the heat.

But I needed more wood. It was gonna get dark. And I'd be alone. With the bears. I tried to swallow the lump of fear in my throat, but it kept coming back up.

Bears. Hungry bears. I wouldn't want to come face to face with one. Where we lived outside of Fairbanks, we'd seen bears on our road a couple of times, once in our driveway, and lots of tracks on the trails my dad made behind our house. When I was little I wasn't allowed to play outside alone. Mom said if we'd lived closer to town it'd be different, but we lived on the edge of wild country, and you never knew what might wander through.

I loaded a few sticks onto the fire, then searched the forest and the top of the beach for more fuel. And I kept running to the shore, scanning the crashing waves, hoping to see the orange of my dad's life preserver bobbing toward shore. Or to see my dad standing, to hear his voice calling to me.

I was on a tiny flat spot of forest. Behind me the land turned steep. It was still forested, but I knew what was above that forest. I'd seen it from the kayak. The granite-capped mountains of Bear Island. And they were steep, like you'd need a rope to climb them.

I crisscrossed some branches onto the fire. I wanted it big.

Dad, I thought. He'd know what to do. Wild country was one of his two loves. My mom was the other.

My dad was kind of a loner. But I didn't realize how much of a loner he was until after Mom died three years ago. I mean, they used to have friends, but really they were her friends. "Your mother had a lot of friends," he would say, "and I had your mother." He felt more at home in the woods than anywhere. That's why my dad moved to Alaska in the first place. That's why we lived ten miles out of town on a big piece of land.

He liked the quiet. Every winter he'd pick a spot farther away from the house down one of the trails he'd cut by hand, and he'd set up a canvas wall tent with a small woodstove. When I was little he'd put me in a sled and pull me out there. "Going for a sled ride, Tom." I loved those rides. Then later, I got my own snowshoes and I'd walk out with him. I'd help him cut firewood, and we'd have hot chocolate, and we'd explore from there, examining tracks, and animal scat, and places where moose rubbed the bark off the aspen trees with their antlers. We were a team. A happy team.

Mom would usually ski out. Sometimes she'd bring part of a story she was writing and would read it to us, or a song she was working on. But after Mom died that wall tent sat folded up in the shed. It's still there. And my dad pretty much sat folded up in the house. But on the drive down to Whittier to start the kayak trip, he said it was time to pull the wall tent back out this winter. That I was gonna have my old dad back. We were gonna be a team again.

I ran back to the shore, searching for him, calling, calling, calling. The gray waves rolled up the beach, matching the color of the darkening sky. He's out there somewhere. Alone. All because of me. My head felt heavy, like it was being weighed down by a big bag of sand and it was taking all my strength to keep it attached to my neck.

I glanced up the beach toward the rocky point. Maybe he'd washed up on the other side of that point.

He had a survival kit, too. Tomorrow I'd get over that point and look for him, but right now I needed to take care of myself 'cause if I didn't I wouldn't even see tomorrow.

I walked back to my fire and loaded more sticks onto it. Then I pulled my spray skirt off and let it drop to the ground. Because I was on shore it hung down to my knees, but in the kayak it stretched around the combing of the cockpit, sealing you in. It was supposed to keep out any water that splashed over the top.

I unzipped my life vest and let it drop on top of the spray skirt. Peeled off my raincoat and rain pants, draped them over a tree branch. Took my pile jacket off, wrung it out and hung it on a branch, then huddled near the fire, thankful that the rain had let up some.

I rotated my body, trying to dry off all over. Steam rose from my drenched long underwear tops and bottoms. I pulled my rubber boots off, dumped the water out of them, took my wool socks off, squeezed what water I could out of them, then put them back on, followed by my boots.

Staying dry is one way to stay warm. Moving around is another way to stay warm. You lose a lot of body heat through your head.

Hat and gloves. I got them out of the other pocket of my raincoat, and put them on.

That image. The last glimpse I had of my dad bobbing in the waves kept replaying in my mind. His wet, hatless head and matted beard. My stomach clenched. It started to burn. I took a breath but it kept on burning.

The popping, crackling fire shot sparks. It sizzled as moisture from the branches above dripped. Darkness came. I crawled back into my rain gear and scooted as close to the fire as I could without actually being in it. I wished this was all a bad dream, but knew it was a living nightmare.

CHAPTER 3

THE NEXT morning my head was pounding. My face was inches from the coals, my mouth dry from inhaling smoke and ash. I tried to swallow, but my tongue stuck on the back of my throat.

I sat up. With a stick, I dug into the black splotch of coals, hoping some were glowing.

No luck.

I stepped out of the forest and scanned the beach for any sign, scraps of the kayak, a piece of gear, the orange of my dad's life vest. I could see for several miles across the water, but the cove I was in, bordered by steep, rocky points, cut off my view of the coast.

I walked north, my clammy rain pants clinging to my long-johns, my kneecaps aching a little less than they did yesterday. My damp socks wrapping my lower legs and feet like soggy moss covering rotten logs. My head pounding with each step.

At the stream, I recognized the wide, bright-green leaves that reached above my waist. Skunk cabbage, I remembered Dad calling it, saying, "Bears eat the roots and deer eat the leaves." A whole mess of it crowded the small stream as it snaked back into the forest.

I lay on my stomach, put my face to the stream and drank—my cupped hands shoveling cold water into my mouth. Each time I swallowed, pain shot up the back of my head like an electric shock.

I rolled onto my back and covered my eyes. Yesterday's accident flashed into my mind. I squeezed my eyes tighter until the scene turned black.

I stayed like that until the cold ground forced me to sit up. I reached into my pocket and pulled out the survival kit. I unzipped the two Ziploc bags, grabbed one of the Meal Pack bars, tore the wrapper, and took a bite and almost spit it out.

"Yuck."

The bar tasted like modeling clay mixed with nuts and raisins. I ate the whole bar, and it seemed to wake up my stomach. It felt emptier now than before I'd eaten it.

I kept walking north, reached the point, and cut back into the forest. My rubber boots slid on the steep slope as I switch-backed my way up, gripping tree branches and brush. Unfortunately Devil's club was one.

"Ouch!" I yelled, as I jerked my hand away from a devil's club stem. Pale green thorns dotted my left hand, just below the thumb. I pulled the thorns out and little red dots grew in their place. Then this stinging sensation crept into my hand. I sucked my palm, then rubbed it, trying to ease the sting but it kept on stinging, like it was on its own schedule. I kept going, pushing through the eye-level, foot-wide palm-shaped leaves, careful not to grab any more stems.

I crested the ridge and worked my way toward the point overlooking the water. In the distance, maybe a quarter mile from shore, lay a series of rock reefs. Waves broke over the jagged rocks, exposing and then covering the spiky formations. In front of the closest reef I saw a head pop up, then another and another. Six sea lions swimming north against the waves. I tasted the Meal Pack bar at the base of my throat and swallowed it down.

The waves. They'd pushed me south of the reef, way south. I mean, where I'd washed up looked four times as far as the straight-line distance to shore, and I'd been swimming straight for shore as hard as I could.

I just wanted my dad to appear on the shore. Maybe a little bruised up, but ready to take charge. To tell me what to do and where to go. And to tell me that everything would be all right. To forgive me for my screw-up. And, if he was hurt, I'd take care of him. Build him a big fire and do whatever it took to help him. My chest tightened and I sucked in a short breath, wanting more air.

He had to be around here somewhere. He was stronger than me, so maybe he'd gotten to shore in more of a straight line while I'd been swept by the waves. He may have been a lost zombie at home after Mom died, but out here he was the expert. He knew his way around the forest and knew what to do in the cold. Forty below, fifty below, even sixty degrees below zero and he would still go out on his snowshoes.

The coast angled northwest. A series of black cliffs and tan headlands two to three hundred feet high, dotted with off-shore rocks stretched to the horizon.

We'd been planning to round the tip of the island, paddle down the other side partway, and then cross back to the mainland. But it was gonna be a long crossing, like seven miles. The crossing at the southern end of the island, where we'd come from, was only five miles.

Only five miles of frigid water. Like we could swim either one. I'd barely made it to shore. Still couldn't believe that I was actually standing here. But if I'd made it to shore, Dad must've too.

"Dad," I called. "Dad. Da-ad. Hellooooooo."

Nothing.

I scanned north for smoke from a campfire. For an orange dot on the shore.

Nothing. My head fell forward. I sucked in another short breath.

Directly below me, in the cove to the north, a large stream poured out of the forest and ran over seaweed-covered rocks.

Stream.

Stream meaning fish.

Fish.

Maybe a salmon stream. And just that thought, that tiny flash in my mind, brought my hunger back up. I wasn't a salmon fan at home, but out here I'd eat salmon 'til I grew scales if I could get my hands on some.

Sometimes the streams are choked with salmon. You can almost grab 'em like the bears do.

Bears. Better be careful.

I just wanted to eat.

Eat.

Eat.

Eat.

Not because something tasted good, but because I was starving. And, maybe Dad was up that creek. Maybe that's why I couldn't see him. Maybe he was catching a fish right now, or cooking one. I sniffed the air for the odor of cooking fish. I couldn't be sure but I thought maybe I smelled something.

Too bad I wasn't fat. Then I'd have some reserves to burn. My eighth grade science teacher, Mr. Haskins, used to joke around about his reserves. He'd pat his belly and say he could outlast any of us in a hunger situation. We'd all laugh, but he'd just stand there, smiling.

Dad had more reserves than me, but he wasn't fat. We were the same height, about 5' 10", but he had more muscle. He was a carpenter and had all those years carrying plywood and beams and flooring. I wasn't super skinny, but you could see my ribs when I didn't have a shirt on. But I was building up some muscle from working with Dad.

After Mom died he started taking me to work with him in the summers. Even then he barely spoke to me unless he had to give me a direction or show me how to do something, but at least I was with him. I started off doing simple stuff like stacking building materials, or coating boards with stain, but I helped with pretty much everything now.

My dad had a degree in biology, but he liked keeping his own schedule, deciding when he would work and what kind of work he'd do. *Just keeping it simple*, he'd say. Too simple, if you ask me. We had a TV that you could only watch movies on.

"Can't we have cable, like Billy does? Like everyone does?" I'd asked.

"When you get your own place you can rot your brain however you want."

And no computer—at least not one that could get you on the Internet. And games in our house, they took place on a board, not a screen. That didn't really bother me when Mom was alive. Then I had someone who'd actually play something with me. We didn't even have a microwave. Walking into our house was like walking into the 19th century. Our porch railing looked like a hitching post for horses.

On the beach, I approached the stream. Partially eaten, rotting salmon corpses lay among the rocks on the shore. Eyeless heads attached to backbones with strips of shriveled gray skin clinging to the skeletons. Nasty stuff all around.

But in the creek was a wall of pink salmon. You could see their humped backs breaking the top of the water. Pinks—Humpies is their other name because of their humped backs—are mostly what's in Prince William Sound, according to Dad.

Grab 'em like the bears do.

I glanced around. Gave my head a shake. The voice sounded so real. Like he was talking into my ear. Maybe that was a good sign. Maybe it meant that he was close by.

I waded into the stream, but everywhere I walked fish swam away from me, hundreds of them. Before I could even get my hands in the water, they were gone.

So then I stood still in the water. In my mind I saw it. I'd scoop my hands under a salmon and just sweep it onto shore. Easy.

Easy.

Easy.

Easy.

But the fish wouldn't come. Wouldn't come near enough for me to even try to grab them.

I walked out of the stream and sat on the beach.

I pulled the survival kit out of my pocket and inhaled the other meal pack bar.

Still hungry, I faced the stream and felt the dead-salmon-stink hit my face.

My stomach growled.

"No. No way will I eat those." I shook my head and looked away, but my eyes kept coming back to the carcasses. Like my stomach had taken over for my brain and was calling the shots.

Then I saw movement across the stream. I stood up. A black bear stood on four legs on the opposite bank just a football field's distance upstream. A distance a charging bear could cover in seconds. I wanted to run but knew that was the exact wrong thing to do. You don't give a bear something to chase. You don't make yourself a running target. Any idiot knew that.

I took a step backward, my heart pounding like a jackhammer. We'd seen a bear the second day of the trip. We stood at the edge of the forest as it nosed around in some tide pools. "Just stand still and watch," Dad had said, his hand resting on his pepper spray. No gun. Dad didn't even own a gun. My best friend, Billy, his dad had, like, five guns. He kept them locked up but Billy said he knew where the key was. I wished I had one now.

The bear walked into the stream. I didn't even know if it saw me. Or if it did, it didn't seem to care, like it was thinking, "Yeah, Tom, what are you gonna do?"

The bear lunged forward and swatted the water with its powerful front paws, splashing water every which way. It plunged its head underwater, then surfaced with a fish bending side to side, flexing with all its might to return to the stream.

The bear settled into the beach grass and dropped the fish. The fish flopped, but the bear just put a paw over it, like a dog does with a bone. It tore into the live fish just below the head, eating one side of it while it was still flopping. With its mouth, the bear flipped the fish over and ate the other side. I watched that bear catch and eat five more fish like it was no big deal. Probably did it all the time.

And for a few minutes I actually forgot that I was hungry, forgot that my dad was missing, forgot that I was stuck on an island in Prince William Sound sixty miles from the nearest town. Yeah, it was all about the bear, and how it lived. How it ate things that were still flopping. Still living. How the fish's life passed into the bear, became part of the bear. Like some of the stuff my mom used to write and sing about. In my mind I saw her guitar sitting in my room. She had some songs she'd started. I was planning on finishing them.

Then a growl from my stomach pushed into my throat, and the hunger kicked back in.

I couldn't catch fish like a bear. Or could I? Could I dive in and grab one, and toss it on shore? But I had stubby fingernails, not sharp claws. And, I'd get soaked.

I could feel the digestive juices creeping up my throat—burning.

I wanted a salmon.

I needed a salmon.

CHAPTER 4

I DIDN'T dare move until the bear moved northward. I watched it disappear into the forest and then reappear several minutes later farther along the shore. Then it climbed the next point and was gone.

Two bald eagles moved in to clean up what the bear had left, along with a flock of gulls.

I walked upstream, opposite of where the eagles and gulls were feeding, found a shallow spot, and crossed. As I stepped out of the water, the gulls squawked and rose, flying down to the shoreline where they resettled at the mouth of the creek. The eagles departed silently, their long wings carrying them skyward.

I faced the carnage. Not much but heads, tails, and bones. Still clinging to the heads of the bear-killed salmon were bite-sized chunks of dull pink meat. Leftovers, but I'd take them.

I grabbed a salmon by the tail. It slipped from my hand into the matted-down beach grass. Fish slime and bear drool covered the carcass.

I wiped my hand on the beach grass. "Nasty."

I hunted around and found five of the six fresh kills. Then I carried them across the creek and downstream to the spot where I had observed the bear. It was out in the open, so I could see if the bear came back or if another one showed up. Or, if my dad appeared from the forest or from up the coast, or even from the way I'd come, I'd see him.

I used another hunk of fire starter stick to get a fire going. I kept adding slightly damp sticks, and turned a steaming mass of wood into a small blaze.

The fire starter sticks, little brown rectangles of solid fuel, were awesome. It was like having a mini-fire to start your real fire. You could focus on getting small sticks to catch over a steady flame.

My dad, he knew his stuff. Without the survival kit I'd be scarfing raw salmon, and probably puking it back up. That is, if I was even still alive. That first fire had kept me from freezing to death, kind of anchored me to my own life. I could've just curled up and let the cold take me.

Build up a bed of coals. Get some green alder branches. It grows just above the beaches. Lay the green alder crisscrossed to make a grill. Put the fish on the grill and cover it with alder leaves. Grilled, smoked salmon. And nothing to clean up.

He wanted to cook a salmon for me like this, but we hadn't caught any. Hadn't fished much, really. My dad really wanted to do an epic trip, that's what he'd said, a big journey. The kind he used to do with Mom before I was born. Said if I liked this trip, then next summer we could do a whole month.

I hadn't said anything. Didn't know if I'd even want to do another kayak trip. I wanted to get my learner's permit and then my driver's license so I could get to town when I wanted. So I could eventually have a freaking life outside our house in the sticks. So I could take guitar lessons and join any school club or play any sport I wanted. So I could do what I want without depending on my depressed dad to get off his butt and take me somewhere. Anywhere. But now, I'd kayak with him the whole summer next year if it meant finding him alive.

When Mom was alive, I didn't feel as isolated because she was always talking to me or getting the three of us to do things or taking me with her when she went to visit Heather's mom.

I missed Heather. We were the same age and our moms were best friends, but they moved away three years ago. Right after Mom died. Me and Heather even used to take baths together when we were little, and I've got pictures to prove it. They're planning on coming back after Heather's dad finishes law school. We get a card every year with a photo. In the last one Heather had her braces off.

A spruce branch bounced up and down just back in the forest. I took a step back, my heart pounding.

"Dad?"

Something dark flickered between the branches.

Bear. I took another step back.

Then two blue-colored birds with black crests atop their heads, flew toward me and landed in a tree closer to the fire.

I let out a sigh. What if that had been a bear?

Take a breath, Tom. Whenever you see something move. Just take a breath, focus and then respond. Alert but calm.

Alert but calm, I thought. It might sound easy but it's not, especially when you hope that every little sound, or movement is your dad, and not some animal that might try to eat you.

Get some green alder.

I turned back to the fire. "Green alder? Screw that. I'm starving. I'll just use the wood I've already collected."

My stomach was an empty pit and I needed to fill it.

I crisscrossed some thin branches on top of the coals and laid the fish carcasses on them. Instead of alder leaves, I ripped handfuls of beach grass from the ground and used them to cover the fish. The beach grass stalks were stiff and about an inch wide.

I heard hissing from under the beach grass. I hoped it was bear drool burning off.

After a few minutes I started to smell cooked fish, a smell that never excited me at home. I spied a little orange flicker under the beach grass. Then the orange reached through the beach grass. I blew on the flames, which disappeared for a moment, then came back stronger. Again I blew, with the same result.

The beach grass caught; it turned black and started to curl. Flakes of ash drifted upward, and a wall of heat hit my face as an explosion of orange and red engulfed the fish. I grabbed a stick and knocked three of the carcasses out of the flames, then snatched the other two by the tails and flung them out, and they sat there steaming and smoking on the rocks.

I touched one and it wasn't as hot as I thought it'd be, so I picked it up by the backbone, turned the charred side toward my mouth and took a bite.

Burnt fish. Not bad. In fact, under the crispy skin it wasn't so burnt, just cooked, even a little juicy, and, seasoned with bear drool. But the unburnt side was still raw, so I gnawed on the charred sides of the other fish, then placed each one back on the coals to burncook the other side. As tasty as it was, I wanted to singe that drool off.

But there wasn't much meat, just a little below the heads, some flakes along the backbones, and a hunk by the tails. I sucked the backbones like a high-powered vacuum cleaner—the kind my dad used on building sites—until every speck of meat was gone. And then I wished for more.

"I want to burncook a whole fish, without bear drool."

A fish that I'd caught.

I crossed the stream and hiked north, along the edge of the forest, calling out for my dad, but I'd strained my voice yesterday and after a while I could barely speak. So I walked just inside the forest dodging Devil's Club, peering behind the trunks of massive trees, hoping to find my dad leaning against one. My heart thumped in my raw chest, my eyes hungry for any sign of him. A scrap of clothing, a paddle, a dry bag.

When I reached the next point, I turned and retraced my steps. Maybe he'd swum to shore south of where I'd washed up. The wind and waves had pushed me south, so maybe he'd been pushed south even farther.

But now, the water was turning gray. And the pale red outline of the sun, barely breaking through the clouds, was sinking toward the horizon. I had maybe a couple hours of daylight left and I needed firewood. Tomorrow I'd climb the steep point south of my cove and keep looking.

I hiked back over the point and rebuilt my fire under the same massive spruce tree, then collected more wood. It started raining lightly. I mean, you couldn't even tell unless you stepped out onto the beach and tilted your head up; only then could you feel the mist on your face.

I dumped some wood next to the fire.

I was already hungry again. And even though I wasn't freezing like yesterday, I still wasn't warm. Warm like I'd been with a tent and sleeping bag. And dry. I still wasn't dry.

I took the emergency blanket out of the wrapper. It was silver and thinner than tin foil but really flexible. You could scrunch it up like a plastic bag and it wouldn't rip. And it was big—seven feet long and about four feet wide.

I draped it over my head and shoulders and pulled it around me like a cape.

But the fire burned down and I got cold, so I shed the blanket, added wood to the fire, and then searched behind camp for more.

I stepped over a rotting log and my foot sank and made a sucking noise, like I'd stepped into deep mud.

Fresh bear scat. A huge mother of a pile.

I twisted my foot out of the crap, then noticed another mound beside it. Now my heart was pounding. I scanned the forest for movement.

"Relax," I said. "Relax." But my heart kept pounding.

I looked at the scat again, and eyed some purple dots mixed in with the dark brown. Whole blueberries. Somehow they'd survived the journey through the bear's digestive system. I didn't want any part of myself making that journey. I glanced around. Gulped some air.

But the berries. I touched my empty stomach.

Food and firewood. I needed both.

"Berries. Okay. I'll eat berries," I said. "I'll eat a boatload of berries— whatever I can find before dark."

I hiked across the slope to a tangled mass of deadfall, where several trees had fallen, one on top of the other, and began pulling branches out, making a pile. I glanced toward camp, then I looked upslope and side-to-side, searching for bears in the twilight.

I scrambled farther up the deadfall and there they were.

Blueberries.

I plucked one from the branch. Dark blue and round. I rolled it around in my hand and popped it into my mouth.

Most blueberries in Prince William Sound have little white worms in them. They really grossed your mother out. She refused to eat them. But it's a good protein source to know about if you need it. And, you can't even taste the worms.

"Worms or no worms," I said. "I'm hungry. Bring them on."

I attacked the bushes, eating every berry in the small patch.

Maybe this is how it is. Move along. Find a berry patch and eat. Fill up your gut with worms. Just like the bears.

There it was again—in my mind—bears.

This place is full of bears. But it's full of food, too. Rarely will a bear prey on a human. Most bear attacks happen to people who are alone. We've got each other.

I pulled more branches from the deadfall and made another pile of wood. I kicked at the ground. We didn't have each other—not right now.

BEFORE THE ACCIDENT

Usually we hugged the shore. That way you had more chances of seeing land animals close-up on the coastline, plus it was safer. But along this stretch, after that group of sea lions left us, we were cruising a couple hundred yards out to avoid an endless minefield of rocks poking up from the bottom. It was my job to spot them.

Off in the distance, I caught a glimpse of a big black fin. I twisted my neck so my dad could hear me. "Over there." I pointed with my paddle. "I think it's a whale."

CHAPTER 5

THE NEXT morning I woke to strands of fog. They reached into the forest and settled around me. I knew I needed to get over that point to the south. It was at least twice as tall as the one to the north and steeper, but maybe Dad was over there. Maybe he was hurt, or looking for me, freaking out because he couldn't find me.

After he found out Mom died, he stood in the kitchen and dropped plates, one by one, on the floor until he'd broken them all. Then he took the bowls and did the same thing. I remember telling him to stop, but he acted like I wasn't even there. I went into my room and cried and cried, and he never came in. When I came out hours later, he was sitting on the couch, and in the kitchen there wasn't a speck of glass on the floor. I sat down next to him, and he put his arm around me. "We'll get through this," he said. But then he didn't say anything much for months and months.

"I'll get through this," I said. "I'll just keep searching for Dad until I find him." Another shiver ripped through my body.

I put my life vest on, folded the emergency blanket and put it in my pocket, grabbed my spray skirt and walked to the water. Foot-high waves broke on the shore. The fog had lifted some, but the point to the south was still covered in a gray-white haze.

At the base of the point there was a patch of blueberries. I ate and ate and ate but was still hungry. My stomach felt raw, like someone had taken a piece of sandpaper to it. Maybe it was the acid from all those berries. And all the tiny white worms swimming around.

I zigzagged my way up into the fog, the gentle lap of the waves in my ears. If only it'd been like this a couple days ago.

My dad had told me about paddling in nine-foot seas, climbing up one side of the waves and down the other. "It wasn't so much the waves but what you did in them, how you responded to them," he'd said.

If only I'd done something different. If only I'd done what I was supposed to do. I stomped on a skunk cabbage plant over and over, smashing the three-foot tall leaves into green mush. Sweat ran down my neck. I stared at the mush, not wanting to move. My sweat cooled and my feet got that feeling, that pre-cold feeling that said, *you better move soon if you want to keep your toes.*

I lifted my head. "Okay, I'll keep going." Even though I didn't want to.

I started to sweat from the climb and unzipped my raincoat. The fog was starting to break up a little more. On top, I picked my way over a few fallen trees and through some prickly Devil's Club to the edge of the point. It was pretty much a straight drop to the rocks below. Maybe three hundred feet. And the point itself was broader than I'd imagined. A big rounded cliff top. I'd have to head inland a little bit to get back down to the water.

I walked along the edge, looking down, and caught a glimpse of blue wedged between two rocks. I zipped up my coat, lay on my belly and squinted. A dry bag. The bag with our sleeping bags. But there was no way to get to it.

I took a couple shallow breaths. Sleeping bags. There was a flashlight in there too. A candle lantern and extra matches. And what else...maybe dry socks, and a couple of spare wool caps?

Then I saw a faded red edge pointing straight up. A piece of the kayak, maybe a couple feet long, leaning against a rock. In my mind I saw my dad bobbing in the waves. I closed my eyes.

"Get out! Out of my freaking brain!" But it wouldn't leave. I repeated the word "black" over and over until all I could see was darkness. My body trembling, I opened my eyes and crawled along, my chin moist from resting against the mossy ground. I saw nothing more besides rocks, but in lots of places I couldn't see directly below because the cliff was undercut. No way to get there unless you had a boat, and even then it'd be dangerous—pointed rocks with waves breaking through them.

The fog rolled back in. At least I hadn't seen any orange trapped on those jagged rocks. I mean, if you spent a day trapped down there after being in the ocean you'd pretty much be toast.

I put my hands on either side of my mouth and called down again and again but heard only the waves like they were pounding on my head every time they broke on the rocks below.

I kept to the edge as much as I could, catching glimpses of the rocks below when the fog let me, then cut inland and started to work my way down to the other side.

I faced the hillside and took backwards-sideways steps while gripping the wet brush for balance.

Side step.

Side step.

Side step.

Then I'd turn and do it again in the opposite direction, snaking my way down the steep, forested slope, keeping my legs bent the whole time.

I stepped onto the beach and straightened my legs. I turned and through the thin fog saw an orange dot at the far end of the cove.

"Oh," I whispered. My stomach clenched and my throat tightened. I swallowed. "Dad!"

CHAPTER 6

I Ran toward the orange, but my legs felt rubbery, like I was gonna trip every time I took a stride, but I kept running and stumbling, caught my toe on a rock and fell, but got up and kept going.

Was he moving toward me? Had he heard me? "Dad! Dad!"

I was getting closer now and I could see the orange vest gently rising and falling, twisting a little right at the edge of the water.

About fifteen yards away I slowed to a walk, then stopped.

"Dad," I whispered.

"Dad!" I yelled.

"No!" I screamed. "No! No! No!" I waded in over my boot tops and grabbed the vest. I looked out at the expanse of water, the waves washing my legs up to my thighs. I remembered my vest riding up on the back of my head, pushed continually by the big waves. I kept grabbing it and pulling it down. But Dad, he could've done that too. He would've done that.

I stepped back and fell onto the beach and buried my face in the vest.

If everything would just stop. Right now. Just stop.

Where was he?

The cold crept in. I forced myself to sit up. I was breathing hard, but couldn't get enough air because my throat was so tight.

I sat hunched over, sucking air in little gasps. Like I was gonna die. Like how I imagined my mom dying.

One summer afternoon Mom went out for a bike ride and never came back. Hit and run. She was gonna bike this loop she always bikes. We live on forty acres outside of Fairbanks, toward the end of the Old Nenana Highway. But the loop Mom biked took her onto the real highway for a few miles and that's where she got hit. Yeah, she had a helmet on but it didn't matter. Some car or truck plowed into her and knocked her down a steep embankment. She'd bled to death. Sliced up by some sharp rocks.

I forced myself to stand up and breathe. My legs shook.

And my feet were ice from going in over my boot tops.

I slammed the vest onto the ground.

My eyes grew hot but no tears came.

That last image of him bobbing in the water popped into my mind again.

I sat down, and pounded the vest.

At the start of the trip, Dad had said, "I want more for you than my father could give me. I want more for us than what I had with my father. And your mother? If she could see us, she'd be happy that we're doing this trip. Going to places she loved. Places that she wanted to take you. And, that I'd finally picked up the ball and started living again. Finally."

My mom. Dead.

My dad. Gone.

I slammed my body back, and let out a scream that shook the clouds.

Where was he? He had finally come back. He has to be alive. If he were dead, I would've found his body on the shore. Wouldn't I?

And then, I thought, maybe he lost his life vest while he was swimming ashore but he still made it to shore. Maybe he'd latched onto a floating dry bag with some of our gear in it and had used that to stay afloat, and now had a bag full of food or clothes, or maybe the tent. Probably better off than me right now. But where was he?

One life to live. My mom had those words on the fridge and my dad left them there. Even though he was like the walking dead after she died.

But this trip. He was snapping out of it. He'd said, "Tom you're gonna have your old dad back if it kills me." Said he'd buy me a new bow. He'd taken the old one and burned it after my mom died. Burned my target up, too. All in silence. I thought he might destroy Mom's guitar when I started playing it, but he didn't. Back then, she was gonna start giving me lessons when school started and, now, he said I could get those lessons with her guitar.

Dad had built a cedar box for Mom's ashes. It sat on a table by his bed. He'd lie on his back with some headphones plugged into an old CD player. Mom had recorded some of her songs, and he just listened to that CD over and over. I'd peek into his room and see him with his eyes closed and his lips moving, like he could just live in his little world, not including me. Like why couldn't we have listened together? I asked once but he didn't even respond. Just shook his head turned away. I was furious then. I mean, I was sad too, but losing her was like losing both of them—until a few weeks ago.

I stood up and started walking toward the trees. The skin of sweat blanketing my body was cooling me. When I reached the thigh-high beach grass I sat down again. My mind was a storm. What now? I hugged the vest to my chest and felt the bulge.

I turned the vest around, put my hands on the bulge, then pulled them away. He had a big zippered pocket on his life vest where he carried his kit.

Eating his Meal Pack bars wouldn't be fair. Then another thought crept into my mind on top of the first one. He'd want me to have them. To have what I need.

I unzipped the pocket and removed the survival kit.

I held one of the Meal Pack bars in my hand. I wanted to tear the wrapper off and scarf it down. Instead, I held it up to my nose and sniffed, and a sickly sweet smell invaded my nostrils. Even though I could eat a dozen Meal Pack bars, I thought, I need to hang on to these for when I find Dad because when I find him he's gonna be hungry.

Then I walked the beach just above the most recent strand line, kicking at the seaweed left by the last high tide.

"Dad, Dad, Dad," I kept calling, searching for tracks in sandy spots, peering into the trees, and scanning the open water, and studying the forest for any signs of him. And I kept my eyes open for anything from the accident that might've washed up. Anything.

At the north end of the beach, the place I'd come down off the cliffs, I turned and retraced my steps.

"Where are you?" I said. "What do you want me to do?"

What would he do if he'd found my vest and nothing more?

And then it hit me. I needed to leave a sign. I hadn't left one where I'd washed ashore, but I'd leave one here. Something so he'd know I was alive. Something big.

CHAPTER 7

I STARTED carrying rocks up the beach and stacking them on top of a huge fallen tree just beyond the beach grass. No tide could touch what I was making. I tried to block everything else out and just get the job done, but that image of my dad bobbing in the water kept invading my brain. I slammed a rock onto the ground in front of the fallen tree. Then I picked up another and did the same thing. I took a breath, felt the heat behind my eyes. The accident was my fault. Just like my mom's accident.

If I would've gone on that bike ride with her we would've stayed on our road because the whole loop was too long for me back then. But I'd said no.

"I want to keep shooting my arrows at the target," I said.

"Are you sure you don't want to go, Tom? It'll be fun." Mom said.

"No, Mom. I don't want to go. Just let me be."

The school counselor told me it wasn't my fault. After a while I agreed with him so he'd shut up and quit talking about it. And sometimes I really believed that I had nothing to do with her dying. But deep down, I still felt responsible. I still felt the ache in my gut. A burning ache.

Just before sunset, as I gathered wood for a fire, I discovered fresh bear scat spotted with whole blueberries.

This place is full of bears.

I turned around and peered into the forest. "Dad," I said. "Dad? Is that you?"

His voice boomed in my brain. I didn't understand it. It's not like I was thinking about what Dad thinks—his words were just popping in there and echoing around whenever they pleased. But maybe it was a sign. A sign that he was out here. Somewhere.

"Sorry, Dad." I hesitated. "Sorry I didn't do my part." I waited. Sort of hoping he'd answer, but heard nothing.

I faced the water and saw a couple of sea lions surface and then dive. I kicked at the ground and then bowed my head. Apologizing didn't make me feel any better, but what more could I say? And what difference would it make?

I stomped off into the forest and collected more wood and ate blueberries as I found them. As the sun set, I watched the high clouds, which had moved in, turn red and orange.

Using dead hemlock twigs and splinters of driftwood, I tried to build a little teepee of dry sticks to start my fire but my hands kept shaking and I couldn't place a stick without knocking over what was already there.

"This is all your fault, Dad." I yelled. "Coming out here was your idea. Not mine."

I grabbed a fire-starter stick and fed it small dry wood and got a fire going even though I wanted to save them for when I didn't have dry wood.

By the firelight, I looked at what I had:

> 2 emergency blankets
> 2 lighters
> 2 small boxes of waterproof matches (40 total)
> 4 pixie fishing lures with treble hooks
> fishing line (two small bundles)
> 2 lock-blade pocket knives with four-inch blades
> 12 small pieces of rope
> 2 small pieces of flint
> 4 two-inch fire starter sticks
> In addition to my own clothing I had Dad's life vest.

But no tent, no sleeping bag, no food—except for the Meal Pack bars, but those were for my dad.

I waited for his voice to come, but it didn't. I hoped for a sign, any sign that would give me a clue to where he was, or what I should do, but none came. I stared into the fire. Faces came and went as the flames curled around fat sticks. Not faces I recognized, just blurry images that kept appearing and disappearing, one fading into another.

As my possessions lay before me in the flickering firelight full of faces, I battled with the thought that no matter how much I wished things were different, I was alone, all alone, and with what supplies I had lay in front of me. And wherever my dad was, right now, he was alone too.

I glanced down the beach to where a small, rocky point jutted out into the water. At the base of the point, where I'd collected some of my firewood, were two enormous trees.

Trees, I remembered. Big trees. "Yes," I said. "Yes."

And now I knew where I had to go if I wanted to have any chance of getting off this island alive. It's the place my dad would go to, too. The Sentinels.

―――

Long red rays from the sun stretched across the water as we paddled into the protected cove on the southern tip of Bear Island. We'd just made a five-mile crossing from the main land.

"Good job on the crossing," Dad said. "You were strong. Didn't die."

"Thanks," I said. We'd been out for over a week and even though my arms were sore, I was getting stronger from the daily paddling, just like Dad said I would.

It was quiet in the cove. Like it was part of a different planet where the only sounds that existed were our voices and the sound of our paddles slicing through the flat water. The cove was U-shaped, about a mile deep with a half-circle of small forested islands protecting the entrance.

Gigantic hemlock and spruce trees dotted the spit we were paddling along, the tips of their lowest branches in the water at the tide line. We beached the kayak, got out and stretched.

"Your mom loved this spot," Dad said. "The farthest from civilization she'd ever been. Let's walk around before we unload. We've got a little time."

"The trees," I said. "They're huge."

"Your mom, she said the trees were like Sentinels."

"Sentinels?" I asked.

"A Sentinel is a guard. A protector. Something that ensures safety."

"Cool," I said, thinking of my mom and the way she saw the world. "It kind of feels like they're watching over the place."

These trees, over a dozen of them, and twice as wide as my arm-span, towered above us, growing right out of the beach gravel and all on this narrow spit of land at the back of the cove. And there was almost nothing growing under them. Maybe I'd write a song about this place. For Mom.

"I'm glad we made it here together. Not just for your mom, but for us."

I nodded. Mom. Sometimes at home it felt like she was in the next room or out in the garden. And here, I almost believed she'd appear under the trees. I could feel her. I wished she would 'cause I knew she really loved me, really wanted me.

"We were gonna tell you together. Really, your mom was, but since she's gone..."

"What, Dad?" I said. "What is it?" I mean, he was springing back to life but was still quiet, and soft-spoken and there was no telling when he'd just shut back down again and it'd be like I didn't exist. If he had more to tell me about Mom I wanted to hear it. I had some of her song lyrics memorized, and I'd started playing her guitar, and I'd read her stories over and over, but I wanted every scrap of information to help keep her alive in my mind.

Dad looked at me, then put his eyes on the ground. "This is the place where we first talked about building a family."

I took a breath. "Did you even want to have a kid?"

Dad turned toward me. "I'm not the kind of guy that would just go out and adopt on my own. But with your mother there was nothing I wanted more than to be a parent with her, to have our own. To have you. I know I haven't been acting like much of a father, but that's gonna change. I promise."

Then he gave me a big hug, the kind of hug my mom used to give me. And yeah, he was acting more like he used to before Mom died, but only since we'd been out here. The real test would be when we got home and I wanted rides into town to go to the movies, or to guitar lessons if he let me start them, or over to Billy's house, or maybe to meet a girl if I was that lucky. And to teach me how to drive. Could my dad drag himself out of bed or off the couch for me instead of just driving into town once every two weeks to buy groceries, 'cause I'd go nuts if all I did was spend time at home outside of school with someone who'd barely speak to me.

After we unloaded the boat and set up camp, Dad was taking me to our water source, this trickle of a stream spilling down a steep bank, when I saw something and said, "Dad, what's that, back in the trees?" I pointed with one hand and walked toward it.

Dad fell into step beside me. "Used to be a sauna way back when—"

"A sauna? It's just a pile of junk." I pointed to the pile of rotting, moss-covered boards and a few plastic five-gallon buckets that lay in a heap.

"The Forest Service was supposed to haul the rest of that junk out of here, but then gas prices shot up and they cut way back on travel, just like the rest of us. Must be a pretty low priority right now. So few people come way out here. A few kayakers in the summer. Occasionally a hunter motors out in the late fall, or early winter. Someone who's willing to spend the money on gas."

I grabbed the end of a two-by-four and it crumbled in my hand, like scrambled eggs.

"Twenty years ago you'd get a handful of people out here in the summer, and during hunting season. Not anymore. And where we're headed from here, it's even more remote. New territory for me. The exposed side of Bear Island. No one goes out there, but after that crossing, I think you're ready."

CHAPTER 8

THE NEXT day I walked south along the coast—the salty smell settling into my nose—with my dad's vest slung over one shoulder. The rocky beach turned into a cliff and I had no choice but to head inland if I wanted to continue south toward the Sentinels.

I glanced back at the fallen tree with the ten-foot-long rock arrow I'd made on top of it pointing south. And just behind it, a seven-foot-tall stick I'd dug into the ground, piled rocks around its base, and then attached the yellow spray skirt at the top.

"Dad. You'll see the arrow, right? You'll know what it means, right?"

But if he didn't see it, at least I'd tried. I mean, I'd searched to the north, and then I'd found his vest to the south. I couldn't just wait here, hoping. I had to go and just hope he was going in the same direction. He could've kept swimming around this cliff and then came ashore.

But here I was—with or without him—stuck on this island. At home with my zombie dad I'd felt isolated, but this was true isolation. Just me and the rocks, the trees, and the rain. No town just ten miles down the road. No school to go to five days a week where I could see people. No phone. No food. No people. No nothing.

I don't think my dad really cared if he ever saw people, but me, the main thing I'd been looking forward to after the first week of the trip was seeing people. That, and taking a shower.

I turned, and clawed my way through the belt of alders that separated the forest from the beach. Stiff branches crisscrossed every which way. It was like working your way through a web of steel cables. But once I broke through, I was in the old growth. My dad loved that phrase. Old growth. To me it sounded kind of nasty. Made me think of my fourth grade teacher, Mrs. Harper, who never clipped her fingernails. They were long and grayish. My back used to crawl, like an army of spiders were moving up my spine, every time she'd set one of her hands on my desk.

But in the forest, old growth meant big. And green. And wet. Like you were in a giant terrarium. I recognized skunk cabbage, and the palm-shaped leaves of devil's club springing from their thorny stems, two of my dad's favorite plants. And blueberry bushes. But the rest of the plants, I didn't have a clue about. Maybe there were more things to eat, there had to be, but I didn't know. There was so much I didn't know.

I knew the names of the trees towering above me. Mostly Sitka spruce and Western hemlock.

Spruce have square needles and hemlock have flat ones.

And from some of the tree branches this light green-yellow, lacy stuff hung, draped like tinsel on Christmas trees. Strands of it two and three feet long.

The northernmost rainforest. The jungle of the north, that's what Dad called this place.

We'd vanished—that's what it'd look like. I don't even know if Dad had told anyone where we were going. He put the chain across the driveway with the no trespassing sign on it when we left. And after the four hundred mile drive to Whittier, Dad hid the truck in an abandoned boat yard to avoid paying the hundred bucks it cost to park in the lot. And instead of using the boat dock—didn't want to pay for that either—we hauled all our gear down this steep bank to a mud-hole of a beach and launched. That's what he and mom used to do. Great plan if you're planning on disappearing.

In some spots the devil's club and skunk cabbage grew so thick you could hide an army tank in it. I kicked at some moss concealing a decaying log. It'd be easy to disappear in the rainforest. Thick green moss covered everything on the ground. Hopefully it wouldn't cover me.

If my dad had crawled into the forest and passed out, it'd be easy to miss him. I thought about going back and searching more of the coastline to the north, but the farther north I went, the longer it would take to get to the Sentinels, and with the way the waves were pounding south the day of the accident, I doubted my dad could've swam against them. He had to be south.

And now the possibility that I might not survive kept hammering me.

I might try and try and try and still I might die. And I might never find my dad. Maybe he'd survive and I wouldn't. Or, maybe I'd survive, but if I never made it off the island, what kind of life would that be? A short one, probably. A short, lonely one.

Alone. Alone. Alone.

"I am alone!" I shouted. "Someone. Anyone. Come and get me!"

Then, out of the corner of my eye, I saw some brush shake. I turned and said, "Dad? Dad, is that you?" I walked toward where I'd seen the movement, calling for him over and over. And then I saw more brush shaking, so I kept going and kept calling, my heart pounding in my chest. I knew I'd find him. Then the black rump of a bear disappeared ahead, the brush bending as the bear continued moving away from me.

At least it hadn't come at me. I turned and retraced my steps and kept going. I'd find my dad if he were on this island. And I'd leave more clues as to where I was going so he could find me.

I was walking next to a waist-high decaying log sprinkled with hundreds of evergreen saplings. Nurse trees, I think Dad called them. All that new life from one dead tree. But what about people?

When people die are they gone for good? Or are they in Heaven looking down on you?

With Mom, sometimes I felt like she was close by. Especially when I listened to her music. This one set of her lyrics just kept coming back to me, maybe 'cause I'd listened to it so many times.

> *Every fire's a ceremony.*
> *Every story's a testimony.*
> *If you pay attention, you will know what the river knows.*

Lots of people believed in heaven and God, but me, I didn't know what I believed. One time before Mom died, Dad and I were out on the deck. He was cooking salmon on the grill, and I was sweeping up a bunch of dead carpenter ants, when these three guys in white, button-down shirts came walking up the driveway. If you took the time to walk up our driveway, you must really want something. I mean, it's like five-hundred feet long and does a big S-curve up a steep hill, and it's out in the boonies.

These guys wanted to talk religion—their religion, whatever it was.

Dad was polite and let them make their introduction and show their pamphlets, but eventually he pointed to the trees and said, "Church of the Earth. That's what I belong to. I respect your beliefs and hope you'll respect mine, too. For me, life is here. Life is now."

As I walked, my raincoat, rain pants and rubber boots mostly shielded me from the moisture covering the plants. But crawling over and under fallen trees, and then climbing up the slope, I began to sweat, and soon was wet from the inside.

When you're wet, the only way to stay warm without a fire or a change of clothes is to keep moving.

"Yeah, yeah, Dad, I remember."

I reached the top of the first ridge and a flat, broken forest lay before me—stands of trees separated by small ponds and wet meadows.

Muskegs. Soggy but pretty. Too wet for trees to grow. Mostly covered in deer cabbage—those ankle-high, heart-shaped leaves about as big as your fist.

Dad loved to kick around in muskegs. He'd shown me the tiny red sundew plants that ate insects, and said if we'd been out here a month earlier we'd have seen all kinds of flowers. And the ponds that dotted the muskegs, some of them covered with green lily pads the size of Frisbees. He talked more on this trip than he had the past three years combined. Not that my dad was ever much of a talker, but Mom could get him to talk. It's like she had some secret key that unlocked him, and when she died that key went with her until he came back out here.

But now. I shook my head. I stared at the blanket of deer cabbage until it turned a blurry green. My jaw felt heavy, like there was a twenty-pound weight attached to my chin. Where was he?

On the edge of the muskeg, I found some blueberries. I ate and ate. Handful after handful of blueberries. Bush to hand to mouth to body.

And my thoughts raced. I wanted fish. I needed fish. I'd get back to the coast on the other side of the cliffs and find a salmon stream and figure out how to catch them. That's where my dad would go, where the fish were. I wished I had a map.

In a kayak if you wanted to get to the end of Bear Island you followed the shore and paddled. But traveling on foot—there were lots of obstacles. Cliffs, swampy muskegs, deadfall, mountains.

I picked more berries and put them into a Ziploc bag from one of the survival kits.

School had to have started by now. I was registered but I was just a name on a list. Billy would call when I didn't show, but he'd probably just leave a message and wait for me to call back. And if he came all the way out to my house, which was unlikely, he'd see the chain across the driveway and the no trespassing sign. Billy had been away most of the summer visiting his grandparents in the lower 48, so I hadn't told him where we were going.

As I crossed the muskeg the wet ground sucked at my boots and kicked up a smell, like boiled eggs. I worked up another sweat and my thermal underwear stuck to me like a second skin.

On the far side of the muskeg I stopped and looked back at my soggy footprints in the blanket of deer cabbage. Trail to nowhere, that's what my prints would look like from the sky. Like an alien had dropped down, walked across the muskeg and then lifted off.

I was here. But here was nowhere. Stranded. My stomach burned. I pictured the worms wiggling around in there. Nowhere to go.

I kept clawing my way up, just wanting to top this ridge and get back to the coastline. A layer of sweat covered my body, so I got chilled every time I stopped to rest or pick berries.

Finally, I broke out of the trees. The land was still pretty steep, but without the tangles of deadfall, the walking was easier. The slope was covered with boulders—like a bag of giant marbles had been spilled from the ridge-top.

I headed for the low point in the ridge, the way that looked easiest. The bottoms of my feet ached from walking in the thin-soled rubber boots, made more for standing in water than trekking through the mountains.

Faint depressions in the tundra, spaced like footprints, stretched out in front of me. I turned around and noticed that the marks my boots made were similar to the depressions ahead of me. In the forest it was hard to see any kind of track unless you were right on top of it, but here, the way the land opened up I could see the fresh imprints of where someone had walked. And only one other person could've made those tracks in front of me. I picked up my pace and followed them. And I thought, yeah, I was right to head toward the Sentinels. Somewhere deep down, I'd known that's what my dad would do too. "I'm gonna catch you Dad. Soon."

At the top of the ridge I stared down a steep mountainside, way steeper than the one I'd come up. The first part was treeless, then below it, the forest started. And beyond the forest lay a huge pear-shaped bay of blue water.

Hidden Bay, I remembered. We'd crossed the entrance early in the day of the accident.

Biggest bay on the island. Ten miles long, and over four miles wide in the middle. Too bad we don't have time to explore it. Next time, we'll go in there. Probably some good salmon streams.

The place was killer beautiful. Like if you had a boat full of supplies and you were in the bay, it would be amazing. But for me, the thing that made this place beautiful, the endless miles of empty mountains and water, was the thing that could kill me.

It'd probably take an hour to paddle across the mouth of the bay, but it'd take me days to walk around it.

Suddenly the Sentinels seemed very far away to me, too far. I couldn't swim across the mouth of Hidden Bay, or any other bay between me and the Sentinels. I'd have to walk if I wanted to get there. But I had to eat, too.

Maybe I'd run into someone before I got there. Another crazy kayaker like my dad, or someone in a boat who didn't care about how much money he was spending on gas. But I knew chances were slim. I mean, the reason my dad wanted to come out here was because no one else did.

I started side-stepping my way down. Slippery areas with rock beneath moss, covered with chest-high Devil's Club, shared the upper third of the mountainside with patches of other plants I didn't recognize. There was a scattering of boulders on this side of the ridge too, and a footprint here and there.

I tried to avoid the slick, mossy areas, but twice found myself crab-walking down, sliding my butt on the moss 'cause I didn't want to fall and get tangled up in Devil's Club.

Finally, I reached the edge of the forest. But it was even steeper, almost like the cliffs on the coast. If I'd had a long rope I would've used it. The trees were small and spread out. And there were lots of blueberry bushes that hung like curtains down the slope, but they didn't have any berries on them.

I tried to dig my feet in sideways, but the rocky ground was just as slick as the slope above. So I started grabbing the berry bushes by their bases for a little balance. I could see downslope where there were more trees. I hoped it'd be less steep, too. Plus I could go from tree to tree when I got there.

But for now it was sidestep, sidestep, sidestep, grab a bush at the base, and rest. Then repeat.

I worked my way around a boulder, and then sucked air into my gut as my foot grazed the rump of a black bear.

The bear twisted away from me and I jumped backwards. My feet scrambled for grip as my arms reached out for the steep slope. I grabbed a berry bush by the base and it gave way. I fell backwards, like I'd been dumped out of an airplane, and landed on my back with my legs flat, pointing downslope. A sea of green flew over me as I bumped down the slope and gained speed with no sign of stopping.

I let out a scream.

Then my heels hit something that sent a jolt through my hips and all the way to the base of my head. I flopped forward, and all of a sudden I was flying through the air. Everything slowed down, like an instant replay of someone doing a ski jump.

I knew I was moving, was airborne, but felt no pressure—no resistance. Then I slammed into the ground. Face first. Mouth first.

BEFORE THE ACCIDENT

The whale stayed in the distance, ignoring us, as we paddled north. But then another group of sea lions swam toward us and Dad turned the kayak further from shore.

When Dad did this, the sea lions corrected their course like we were a target they'd locked in on. I kept on paddling, my head cocked over my left shoulder watching them close in on us.

"Keep it steady," Dad said. "I've paddled through herds of them lots of times and nothing has ever happened. But the way that first group nudged the kayak—as much as I like seeing them, I wish they'd just leave us alone."

Now they were twenty yards away and one of them surfaced with a salmon in its mouth. It shook its head back and forth, tossed the stunned fish into air, and swam after it. The other sea lions dove. Maybe they were all fishing. I mean, if given the choice between harassing kayakers or eating, they'd probably choose to eat.

"That'll keep them busy." Dad said. "We need to work our way back toward shore."

CHAPTER 9

WHEN I tried to breathe, I felt all these sharp pains, like when I was helping Dad build a deck and my stomach slammed into the end of a beam and knocked the wind out of me, only this was a hundred times worse.

I rolled onto my side and curled up, my whole body trembling, like how a dog quivers when it's scared.

I lay there until the trembling died down and I could breathe without all the pain.

I lifted my head, then moved my arms and legs. They seemed okay. I sat up. That's when I noticed the taste in my mouth.

I spat some bloody saliva, ran my tongue between my teeth and lower lip, and felt two flaps of flesh where there shouldn't have been any. And under the flaps, I poked the tip of my tongue into two deep gashes.

I spit more blood. The gashes stung, like pieces of hot metal were pressing into them.

If my mouth had been open when I'd hit the ground, I'd have broken my teeth.

Check everything. Carefully.

I pressed a finger onto my bottom lip and it came back bloody. I wished I had a mirror. I mean, I didn't know if the blood was from the gashes, or someplace else. I pulled my lip out and curled it down, trying to see the damage, but that didn't work 'cause my nose blocked my view.

I ran my hands across my face but didn't find any more blood. My lip felt tight, like I'd been punched in the mouth by the mountain. And my cheeks on both sides of my nose just below my eyes screamed with pain.

I lay back down on my side and pulled my knees to my chest. I was never gonna make it to the Sentinels.

My sweat cooled and I started to shiver.

Get up.

"Shut up." I waited but didn't hear anything in response. "Good." I said. "I don't want you whispering crap into my ear. You say almost nothing for three years. You can't just turn it on and expect everything to be okay." Another shiver ran through my body. The bottoms of my feet were going numb.

"Okay," I told myself, "If I just lie here, I'll die for sure. And, what if I don't find my dad? I make it to the Sentinels but he doesn't? What then?"

Live in some kind of home for the homeless?

Or with my uncle and his family in Michigan? I'd seen him once my whole life. He came up after Mom died. Tried to talk my dad into doing some kind of religious ceremony. Said there was still time to *save* my mom.

Take one day at a time. One moment at time.

I sat up and put my hands on my ears. "Shut up. Just shut up."

I stood, and pain shot through my right hip.

Bruises. Just bruises. But in my mind I saw a broken leg. A broken arm. And bleeding, lots of bleeding. No one to help me.

And then I thought about my dad. If he was down there in Hidden Bay and I just gave up, then what would happen to him? If he lost me, it'd just send him over the edge again. My chest tightened. "I'll find you, Dad. I'll make this right."

I used baby-steps to pick my way down the last of the steep section, my hip throbbing with every step. I kept glancing over to both sides and behind me. I mean, not that long ago I'd kicked a sleeping bear, and yeah, it'd run away, but it could be anywhere. Bears weren't as scary when they ran away, but still, if that bear had wanted, it could've had me for lunch. Could've pinned me down like a flopping salmon.

Then I was working my way through flat forest, dodging deadfall and fighting brush, and I heard a twig snap behind me. I jerked my head around and jumped backwards.

I caught a glimpse of a squirrel clinging to the side of a spruce tree; then it dropped to the forest floor and disappeared into some deadfall.

No way, I thought. No way could that little animal make such a loud sound.

Then I remembered what my dad had told me around a campfire early in the trip.

—

"It was on my first solo kayaking trip," Dad said. "It was light out and I was in my tent, reading. I kept hearing something walking in the forest. I'd unzip the tent, stick my head out and have a look around. I did that three times in less than twenty minutes. And each time I heard the walking noise, it sounded louder than before. I was drifting off to sleep when I heard it again, and this time it sounded like it was right on top of me. I panicked, shouted to scare whatever it was away, and blew on a whistle I carried. I was sure it was a bear."

"What was it?" I asked.

Dad smiled. "I got out of my tent, looked around, and didn't see anything. Got back in and heard it again. I thought I was going crazy. I got out and looked again. And then I saw it. And I didn't know that it was responsible for the noise I was hearing until it moved, and I heard a watered-down version of the walking noise."

"What was it?" I asked again, wishing he'd just tell me.

"I'm kind of embarrassed to say—it was a big black stinkbug perched on top of the rain fly of my tent, and every time it moved it sounded like footsteps. The sound was magnified in the tent. And, since I was alone, I was more sensitive to noises and what might be making them."

"A stinkbug," I said, smiling. "No way."

"When you are alone in the wilderness, everything is magnified."

—

The next day I hiked toward the back of Hidden Bay, where the biggest mountains were, eyeing the ground for tracks, or any other sign from my dad. I stopped a couple of times and made rock arrows above the strand line, pointing toward the back of the bay. Pain stabbed my hip with every step and bend and twist. The wounds in my mouth stung, my cheeks ached, and the insides of my arches burned with blisters.

I remembered those bear-killed fish.

A stream. All I wanted was one stream, full of salmon.

What I really wanted was steak and chicken and mashed potatoes and gravy, and some chocolate ice cream.

I'd settle for salmon, but worried about how to catch them. I mean, walking around in that creek and having all those fish swim away from me. That sucked. Like the whole world had abandoned me.

And I couldn't live on bear-killed remains. I'd be like a seagull, waiting for the bears to finish their meal, and then moving in. Except gulls could cross the mountains in minutes, and go from stream to stream scavenging. I didn't have that kind of range. I had to learn how to catch them.

Your mother and I would go to watch bears catch and eat salmon. Those big creeks coming down out of the mountains. That's where they're most likely to be. That's usually where the salmon streams are. Usually. We'd just float in the kayak and watch.

From the top of a headland, I saw the signs of a salmon stream. Yellow-green, seaweed-covered rocks dotted with gulls at the mouth of the creek. As I walked down the slope, I spotted three bald eagles perched in the tree tops. The creek spread out and split into a few channels before flowing into the bay.

Yes.

Yes.

Yes.

I stopped at the first channel. The water was shallow, just shin deep. No fish. So I waded across.

I tromped up one channel and down the next. Covered them all, shallow and deep, but found not one salmon, dead or alive.

At the far side of the last channel I shouted, "Not fair!"

I raised a big rock over my head and slammed it into the creek. I took a deep breath and paced back and forth on the gravel bar bordering the stream. I grabbed another big rock and slammed it into the water.

I pictured the creek where I'd scavenged the bear-killed salmon. The one in front of me looked just like it. And why were the eagles hanging around if there were no salmon? They weren't stupid, like me. They actually lived here. They knew where the fish were.

All day I'd been thinking about the fish. Even slime-covered remains with bear drool a quarter-inch thick would do. Something I could cook on a fire. Something that would stay in my stomach to let me know I'd eaten. The worm-filled blueberries would be good to fill in around the fish, or to eat as I found them, but I couldn't live on them, not with all the walking in front of me.

I let out a scream that emptied my lungs of air, stomped my feet on the ground, and then sat down and cried.

At first I cried like a little kid who wasn't getting his way. But soon I was crying for my dad—where was he? And for my mom, for her short life. And because I knew that with every failure to find food, the chances of ever seeing anyone again grew slimmer.

Six days since the accident or was it seven, I wondered, as I wiped tears from my eyes.

Fish once, two Meal Pack bars and berries, lots of berries. My stomach let out a growl that could've scared a bear away.

"Food," I said. "This is my biggest problem. And I need to fix it." My mind churned away, trying to solve it. Like if I thought hard enough an endless supply of burgers and fries would just appear. A chill ran up my spine. The cold ground sucked the heat out of my legs.

I picked myself up and started for the trees in search of firewood and a campsite.

———

I draped my sweat-soaked socks on the tops of my boots close to the fire, thrilled that it wasn't raining. I was sitting barefoot atop one of the life vests, letting my blistered feet air out. The wormy blueberries I'd eaten sat in my stomach like a tiny puddle on the bottom of an empty swimming pool.

In my mind I started a song like my mom would've done. She made songs for every thing.

> *Wormy blueberries will help.*
> *But alone will only make me yelp.*
> *Like a dog without enough to eat.*
> *Salmon for the Sentinels can't be beat.*

I know my mom could've come up with something better, but she'd be happy that I was making a song. A song with her in mind. "Let the music flow through you," she'd say. "Play with it. You don't make mistakes when you make music. You make discoveries."

There had to be a salmon stream farther back in the bay. Had to be, or else I'd have to cut off some fingers and roast them. Maybe I could work that in.

So the whole thing would go like this:

> *Wormy blue berries will help.*
> *But alone will only make me yelp.*
> *Like a dog I need more than a treat.*
> *Salmon for the Sentinels can't be beat.*
> *If I don't find any, then fingers I'll eat.*

By the firelight I took one of the four, identical, big pixie lures—a silver spoon with a bumpy pink center with a treble hook dangling beneath—from its package. Spawning salmon don't bite, I remembered. They've stopped feeding.

> *Spawning salmon don't bite, but I do.*
> *When I catch one I'll chew and chew.*

That could be the next verse to my rotten little song.

I searched my firewood pile and chose a branch still covered with bark and about six feet long that I could just get my hand around.

The word. What was the word? Hook on a pole. We used one when Dad took me halibut fishing when I was little. Besides me puking into a bucket, I remembered the guide slamming a pole into the halibut.

"Gaff!" I said. "I'm gonna make a gaff!" Yeah, talking to myself again. Or to the world. To anyone who would listen. And singing to the bears so they would know I was here and to go find their own spots.

> *Wormy blueberries will help.*
> *But alone will only make me yelp.*
> *Like a dog I need more than a treat.*

46

Salmon for the Sentinels can't be beat.
If I don't find any, then fingers I'll eat.
Spawning salmon don't bite, but I do.
When I catch one I'll chew and chew.

I pulled out one of my knives, put my hunger aside, ignored my aching hip, sore mouth and blistered feet, and worked the bark off one end of the branch just enough so the lure fit into the barked-out area with hook attached to it hanging off the end of the branch.

Then I took a small piece of rope, wrapped it around the lure and branch three times, and tied it. I grabbed the hook, and pulled. The lure slid partway out of the rope's grip.

"Not good enough."

I sang my new song a few more times. It still sounded pretty bad, but at least it was something. Something I'd created.

I piled more wood on the fire, and kept working on the gaff. Planning ahead. For a time when there would be fish.

That's what grownups do, I thought. They plan ahead.

Their plans didn't always work out, but at least they were prepared to try. I focused on the fire and remembered my favorite of Mom's lyrics, and once they were there, they just kept running through my head like background music:

Every fire's a ceremony
Every story's a testimony
If you pay attention, you will know what the river knows.

Her words sounded way better than mine, but she'd had more practice than me.

I don't know how long I worked at it. I didn't have a watch and it was just plain dark beyond the firelight, but I had finally made something that I thought would work.

With the lure secured by rope in the barked-out area, I'd threaded fishing line through the eyehole at the end of the lure opposite the hook. I'd wrapped the line around the branch and ran it up to the top of the pole. Then I'd tied it in a notch I'd made with my knife.

I hoped the fishing line would keep the lure from sliding up and down, and the rope would keep it from swinging back and forth.

Just within the boundary of the firelight, I sunk the hook into the trunk of an alder tree, and pulled. The line gave a little, but held. It was gonna work. It had to work.

All I needed now were some fish.

CHAPTER 10

FISH. Thousands of fish, I hoped.

I'd walked in the mist all day and had crossed some small streams, but now I was perched on a rocky outcrop above a big creek at the back of Hidden Bay. The creek poured out of some craggy mountains spotted with snow. Islands of yellow-green seaweed separated several stream channels flowing into the cove.

My empty stomach burned with anticipation. I knew I'd starve if I ate only berries.

Fish, fish, fish. I needed fish.

The rush of flowing water filled my ears. Gaff in one hand, I scrambled down from the headland and walked the shore towards the creek,.

In the disappearing daylight, I checked the first of several channels and found nothing. Not even dead salmon. My dad said there were over nine hundred salmon streams in Prince William Sound. This just had to be one of them.

I crossed two more shallow channels with no sign of fish, and trudged upstream on a gravel bar, my blistered feet burning with every step.

Gulls squawked as they lifted off the ground and flew away from me.

I approached the main channel and stopped. Dorsal fins, small triangles poking out of the moving water, swaying back and forth, pointed upstream. I took a step forward and they all moved across the channel and downstream.

Fish all piled on top of one another.

The school was as big as a full-sized pickup truck. Like Dad said: You really could walk across their backs and stay dry if they didn't move.

I pictured the empty creek yesterday and gripped my gaff harder. I needed to understand this. I couldn't just stumble around in the forest and eat berries until I was too weak to walk. There was so much I didn't know. And this was a chance—a chance to know something. A chance to discover. A chance to survive.

I stood like a statue. I had to do this, and do it right.

When Dad took me dip-netting for salmon on the Copper River the summer Mom died, he had said, "Picture the fish swimming into your net."

The Copper River was so full of silt that you never saw a fish swim into your net, you only felt it. You try to hold a net the size of a big trash can in the water on the end of a twelve-foot-long pole. You just feel a thump and haul your net out. But it was like pulling a net through wet cement.

Dad had said, "If I can imagine feeling the bump and then lifting, then I'm ready to dip net." That year we netted thirty salmon in two hours. A week later Mom was dead.

The fish moved upstream, approaching where they'd been before I'd spooked them. In another wave the fish advanced to their original position. I bounced on my toes and that made my blisters burn even more.

Do it and do it right. But how did I know what was right? I just had to feel it. Try it. Imagine bringing the gaff down and tugging. Yanking a fish onto the gravel bar, then pounding it with a rock.

The salmon were headed upstream to spawn—that was their goal. And not up just any stream, but the very stream where they'd had their start as eggs. Well, they weren't all gonna make it. Not if I could help it.

I raised the gaff with both hands, held it over my head, then swung it down, hard. A splash and wave erupted on the water's surface.

"I got one! I got one!" I shouted, as I pulled a fish from the water.

On the gravel bar the fish flopped wildly, and broke free from the hooks. I dropped the gaff, scooped both hands under the fish and flung it away from the water. It hit the rocks and kept flopping and flipping, then became still. I picked up a grapefruit-sized rock, grabbed the fish just above the tail and smashed it on the head. Spasms ran up and down the fish. It broke free and flopped again.

I gripped it by the tail and hit it a second time. It jerked once, then became still. Blood ran from its bulging eyes.

I picked up my gaff. I wanted more. I could scarf down three or four salmon, or eat a whole school, no problem.

I had the situation under control. I was doing it right. It was almost easy.

I waited. The school of salmon moved back to its original position. I swung again, connected again, and yanked, but then stumbled and fell backwards.

Broken ends of fishing line trailed off the pole.

"No," I said. "No. No. No."

I raised the hookless gaff over my head and slammed it down. I stood up and kicked the gaff. I picked it up, stared at the place where the hook should have been, and slammed it to the ground again.

"Worthless," I shouted. "I'm worthless."

Then I felt the trembling. If I kept losing hooks, I'd starve. And that would be sad, loserville-sad—to starve when there were lots of fish just because I couldn't figure out how to catch them.

———

That night, by the fire with a burncooked fish in my belly, I sat with the hookless gaff in my hands, the broken ends of fishing line hanging in the firelight.

I knew I needed to catch more than one fish with one hook. I'd die if I couldn't do that. No room for mistakes. Or at least, no room for making the same mistakes. I needed to learn from this.

> *Learning life's lessons sure can be hard.*
> *You can't learn nothin' if you don't leave the yard.*

Yeah, more of my mom's lyrics. My mom would say that by gaffing a salmon I'd left the yard. But now, if I just tied another hook onto the end of the pole without changing the way I did it, that'd be like staying in the yard.

I set the pole down. I lay back on the life vests and covered myself with the emergency blankets.

I worried about the gaff some more, but no solution came. I'd been so proud of how I'd thought it up, built it, and then caught a fish. I wanted the gaff to work just the way it was, but knew that was impossible. Just like I wanted to have not screwed up on the day of the accident—impossible.

CHAPTER 11

MY EYES opened, then closed again. Then opened. I saw my dad bobbing in the green waves, then his life vest washing ashore.

Then I saw it all again. I closed my eyes tight, then opened them again and saw the gray morning light through the trees.

Then I remembered the fish, the gaff, the hook.

I shivered.

My head hurt, pounded like someone was beating on it with a club.

And my throat was dry, like it was coated with sawdust.

A thin wisp of smoke snaked upward from a partially burnt log. I rolled the log over and stirred the coals beneath it. A few red embers glowed, holding a sliver of last night's blaze.

I placed a couple of small sticks on the coals, blew until the smoke started to rise, then headed for the creek.

Small drops of cold rain dotted the cove as I squatted beside the creek, cupped my hands and drank. The peaks at the back of the bay were blocked by a wall of gray, the clouds closing in on me like a pack of hungry wolves.

I headed back to my camp. A couple life vests, the two small survival kits, plus a fire—that was camp.

I rubbed my hands together. If only I could've reached that dry bag with the sleeping bags. Then at least I'd have something to separate myself from the weather. A cocoon I could curl up in.

I really wished I had a tent. Just a small tent—sleeping bag not included—to shed the rain.

On the trip I'd felt cooped up when we stayed in the tent for a couple days during a storm. It had sucked. I wished it sucked like that now.

If you don't have what you want, what can you do to work toward what you want?

"What do I want?" I said. "What do I want? I want to find you. I want to get off this freaking island! But right now, right now, I just want to live. I want to be warm and dry. And I want to eat—all the time."

My stomach growled. Eat some berries first, I figured. Then build a shelter. Then fix the gaff. And just keep moving around, that'll help keep me from freezing. And keep searching for signs. Any signs that my dad might have left.

On a hillside I found berry bushes, their stems stripped of leaves, a stray berry here and there. And bear scat. Big piles of bear scat speckled with purple and sprinkled with green. Those bears must eat tons, literally tons, of berries. Eating machines.

But the island was big, too big for bears to eat all the berries. I worked my way across the hillside until I found a patch the bears had missed.

The berry juices stung the open wounds in my mouth.

I shoveled them in anyway, but kept my eyes and ears on stand-by.

My dad climbed to the top of a mountain on one of his trips out here and counted nine black bears foraging for blueberries on the mountainside below him. At the time I thought the story was cool. I'd wanted to climb a peak and see that. But now, it freaked me out.

Were any bears moving my way? Was one just out of sight behind a fallen tree? So much to worry about when all I wanted to do was eat.

Eat.

Eat.

Eat.

Not like at home where I used to read and eat, or watch a movie and eat. Eat when I wasn't even aware I was eating.

Especially after Mom died. For a while I just ate what I could. I mean, Dad was down, way down. I'd make him a sandwich when I was making one. And I'd do most of the cleaning up, which was good because I needed something to do.

We had a freezer full of salmon, but he wouldn't touch it. Mom had freezer-wrapped all of it and labeled it with smiley faces and the date, and on the freezer paper had drawn little stick figures of me and Dad fishing. And she'd done all that just a few days before she died. I know it's still there because every once in a while I'd open the chest freezer just to look at those drawings. Everything was there, behind that chain with the sign that said, No Trespassing.

But out here, you take a good look around. Eat for a few minutes. Take another look around.

Eat.

Look.

Eat.

Look.

And listen.

Always listen.

And while I ate and looked and listened, my mind pounded with one word: Shelter.

Shelter.

Shelter.

Shelter.

I worked my way through more berry bushes that had been stripped by bears, searching for another patch they'd missed. I was dodging more mounds of bear scat when I noticed a pile that was smashed in the middle. My mind flashed to the bear scat I'd stepped in my second night stranded on the island. I found an undisturbed pile, stepped in it and studied the result. It looked just like the smashed down pile. It was a print. A boot print.

"Dad!" I yelled. "Dad." I kept moving through the bushes calling for him. I mean, who else could've made that track. And he'd be looking for berries just like me.

I didn't see any more tracks and no one answered my calls. Maybe he was just out of shouting distance. And, he would come to the stream because the fish were there.

I returned to my sorry excuse of a camp.

Don't sleep where you eat. Keep your kitchen separate from your bedroom. Keep a clean camp. Don't give a bear a reason to be interested in where you sleep.

I stood next to the smoldering fire. I knew I couldn't build my shelter here—with the fish-smell. Didn't want to be easy prey or I'd never reach the Sentinels.

But I also knew that I needed to stay here for a little while. I mean, a creek full of fish. If I could stuff my face for few days, build up my strength, then I could make a push for the Sentinels. Plus, this is exactly the kind of place my dad would search for, too. Where there was a food source. That print just had to be his.

Just above the highest strand line, shielded by a band of alders, I discovered an earthen bank about eight feet high. It was kind of dark beneath it because the alders were so thick, but it was a solid wall.

I studied the bank, trying to imagine a shelter.

BEFORE THE ACCIDENT

"Dad, there's a rock straight ahead. Go right."

"Thanks, Tom."

The boat swerved and we glided by the pale green rock peeking out from the trough of a wave. We hadn't seen a sea lion in over an hour.

We rounded a point and the wind hit us straight on. I pulled harder and kept licking the salty spray from the waves off my lips while keeping an eye out for more rocks poking through the surface, and for more sea lions and whales.

CHAPTER 12

I DRAGGED five large deadfalls to the edge of the bank and slid them over, about two feet apart from each other. I gathered sticks and branches, and placed them every-which-way across the deadfalls to make a roof. Something to get me out of this constant rain.

I hauled a bunch of rocks from the beach and built fire rings half-in and half-out of the shelter on the two open-ended sides.

Then I sat inside and tested it out.

Yeah, it was damp and dark. Cold, too.

Just a triangular cave—dirt wall, stick roof, moss-and-mud floor. I hoped it'd feel different with a couple of fires blazing. And I knew I could make it better. Water was already dripping through the roof. But if I spent all my time on the shelter, it'd just turn into a tomb.

I wasn't Mr. Skinny when I started this trip, but I was now.

My clothes hadn't magically gotten bigger, but they hung on me.

And my face? I'd seen my reflection in a puddle yesterday. It looked like it'd been stretched, the way it'd appear in one of those fun-house mirrors.

I scavenged for more berries between my shelter and my kitchen, but they were play food compared to the fish.

At my kitchen I grabbed my gaff, and life vests, and headed back to my sleep shelter.

Energy. It takes energy to make things happen. Sometimes it takes a big push to break through to another level. Rome wasn't built in a day.

His voice just boomed out loud or whispered in my ear with no warning. And the words weren't always things I'd heard him say before. Was he really speaking to me?

When I heard his voice I missed him even more.

And then I thought about home, and if I made it off this island but never found him, just what would be my home? And what was happening at my house now? Was anyone trying to figure out where we were? Would they notice that the kayak wasn't under the deck? Not unless they knew it was there in the first place. Had anyone even bothered to ignore the chain across the driveway and go up to the house? But even if they had, what clues would they find?

My hands had nicks and cuts from yanking and dragging bark-covered branches. The tips of my fingers throbbed, my fingernails packed with dirt and bits of bark. My blistered feet stung with every twist, turn, and squat.

And my shrunken stomach called out for food. I'd worked so hard, but still I had no food, no fire, no gaff. All I had was a cold, leaky shelter. A place to die.

━━━

That night I sat perched on a life vest between two fires, still in my raincoat because of the drips and drizzles that penetrated my shelter.

The other life vest and emergency blankets lay in a pile.

An image of my dad bobbing in the waves invaded my brain. I took some deep, slow breaths and tried to picture Dad before the accident. Before the trip turned bad. His quiet smile. Kind of crooked on one side of his mouth. Just like mine.

I knew he'd be proud that I'd caught a fish and built a shelter. "It's big enough for both of us, Dad." And that I hadn't eaten the Meal Pack bars from his survival kit even though I thought about eating them like three-hundred times a day. And that I'd even thought of trying to go to the Sentinels. I glanced toward the bag holding the combined survival kits.

Dad would take care of what he had. Wouldn't waste anything. At home and on building sites he backed screws out of old boards and reused them. When he cut a tree down for firewood, he used the whole thing instead of just chucking the small branches.

I wondered what he was doing now. Maybe he'd found some of our gear. Maybe he had some matches or a lighter or a fishing pole. Maybe he had the tent. Maybe he had some of our food. The graham crackers and chocolate bars. The marshmallows. My mouth watered and my empty stomach burned, trying to digest itself.

I picked up the gaff.

Make it better, I thought. Stronger.

"A fish is gonna pull, and I need to be able to pull back."

I took a lure from the kit and threaded fishing line through the eyehole.

I tied a knot in the line, creating a small loop, then cut the remaining line, and kept cutting and tying until I had five loops through the eyehole. With a piece of rope I tied the lure onto the gaff so the hook hung over the edge.

I ran a piece of rope through all five loops, wrapped it around the pole and tied it.

I wrapped another piece of rope around this rope and tied it.

Then I took a fourth piece of rope and wrapped it around the fishing line, hoping to hold the lure in place in as many ways possible.

I pulled on the hook—it held. I stepped outside and sunk the hook into an alder trunk just inside the ring of light, and pulled. The hook started to bend.

I smiled, then whispered, "That lure isn't going anywhere."

CHAPTER 13

THE NEXT day gray puffy clouds scudded across a blue sky. No rain, but the northerly breeze crawled up my sleeves and down my neck. Cold. Just plain cold.

But I'd noticed something. Rain clouds came from the south and stayed until a wind from the north blew them away.

Patterns. Weather patterns. Back in Fairbanks, who cared if it was forty below in the winter when you had a warm house to hang out in or all the right clothes to go outside if you wanted to? You didn't really need to deal with the weather unless you lived in it.

You only needed to pay attention to the things that were threatening you. I mean sure, you paid attention to other things, but you didn't have to.

Out here, I needed to pay attention to everything. Like where I put my feet so I didn't fall. Was the hook secure on my gaff? Was a bear following me? Did I have enough firewood to at least last the night? Little mistakes could turn into big mistakes. Like my dad said, when you're alone in the wilderness, everything is magnified.

I headed for the creek, ready to try my new gaff. At my kitchen, the coals from my cook fire had been scooped out and scattered. A pile of bear scat dotted with blueberries crowded the tree I'd slept under that first night.

We are all potentially food for something else.

Okay, okay, I thought. All part of the cycle. Everything is made of recycled nutrients. Berries, bears, people. And once you're dead, you're just a pile of nutrients.

Like, if I died out here, what happened to my body wouldn't matter. Bears would chew on me. Gulls would peck my eyes out. Bugs would gnaw on me. Flies would lay their eggs. They'd hatch, and the maggots would feed.

I kicked the bear scat out from under the tree. This was still my kitchen. I wouldn't turn into bear food—not without a fight.

I stopped to look and listen, then stepped out of the forest, squatted by the stream channel and drank.

I forded the first two channels, then walked across the gravel bar to the main channel, anxious to pull a struggling salmon from the stream. I scanned the water for signs of movement. For swaying dorsal fins.

But all I saw was empty water. I squinted at the channel, like if I looked hard enough, they'd magically appear.

"Where are they?" I said.

I glanced upstream. I wanted to fish out in the open. Where I could see. I didn't want to go up the creek, and be closed in by trees and brush. But there had to be some fish up there. That's where they spawn. But there had to be bears, too.

A cramp ran through my abdomen. I took a step upstream. My chest felt raw. Like I was breathing in tiny fragments of glass. The next couple lines of my mom's song about leaving the yard ran through my head.

> *It might be scary, especially at the start.*
> *You've gotta take that step. You've gotta have some heart.*

Where the gravel bar ended and the channels came together, the water ran deep. I backtracked a ways, crossed the side channel and followed it up to the same spot on the stream bank. In the beach grass I saw the rotting remains of bear-killed salmon.

Make noise to let the bears know you are there, especially if you can't see very far. The last thing you want to do is surprise a bear in a tight spot.

"Hey bear! Hey bear!" I called as I continued upstream, using the same phrase my dad used.

The beach grass ended and I entered the forest. The rush of the water seemed louder, echoing off the trees. My mom's lyrics about having heart kept popping into my head.

I'd taken like ten steps up the creek and was ducking under a fallen tree, when I heard a big splash. I jumped backwards, the back of my head slammed into the tree and I fell on my face. My teeth dug into the wounds in my mouth, and I tasted blood.

I rose to my knees.

"Hey bear! Hey bear!"

I stood up and rubbed the back of my head and spit bloody saliva. If a dead tree could take me out, I really didn't stand a chance against a bear.

There were no bears to be seen, but I made out the shape of a fish at the bottom of a deep pool. I raised the gaff and slammed it into the water but missed the fish, which moved but stayed in the pool. I nosed the gaff into the water and tried to ease the hook under the fish and pull, but the fish kept evading me.

A steady ache settled into the back of my head. I spit more bloody saliva, rinsed my mouth with creek water, and kept crawling over and under downed trees, bashing through brush, and shouting "hey bear," hoping to find a better spot.

I rounded a bend, and a flurry of movement burst upwards. My heart jumped to my throat as a bald eagle took flight from the bank.

I just assumed every surprise movement was a bear. I mean, how could I not? I wanted to be ready. But why did I have to jump backwards? And why did my heart have to beat so hard? Could I teach myself to relax?

To be alert but calm?

Well, I had the alert part down. I was like one of those smoke detectors that beeped when you boiled water. We had one of those. The fire department gave it to us. It was supposed to be really good. After a couple of days my dad took the battery out of it because we couldn't boil water without it beeping.

I rounded another bend. In water about four feet deep, half a dozen salmon, all facing upstream, sat in the bottom of the pool. The water ran shallow over small rocks where it flowed into the pool from upstream.

One fish sprang forward and powered over the rocky area, then disappeared upstream.

Perfect, I thought. Fish runs over shallows and I snag it like a bear.

So I waited, crouched by the shallow spot, ready to gaff the next fish to attempt the run.

I don't know how long I waited, maybe five minutes, and none of those fish moved. My fingers were going numb, so I rubbed my hands together.

I didn't want to put my gloves on and get them all slimy if I gaffed a fish and had to grab it.

So, I just kept waiting, rubbing my hands, wiggling my toes because they were getting cold too.

"Come on, fish," I said softly. "You know you want to try it."

Still, no fish.

How long would a bear wait for a fish? A bear might not wait. A bear might just go into the water and try. Stick its head under and go for a fish.

Think like a bear, I thought. I knew I wasn't gonna dive in, but maybe I could get one in the deep water. This water wasn't quite as deep as the pool downstream where I'd bashed my head.

So I moved to the side of the pool. I focused on the closest fish, raised the gaff parallel to the water and swung it down. The fish scrambled, four of the five disappearing downstream, the fifth jetting up through the rocky area.

"I just can't win! I gotta catch a fish!"

Patience. Remember what you do and don't have control over.

"Shut up," I shouted. "Just shut up!"

I have control over how I act, not over how the fish act. They're trying to survive, too. But I needed one. At least one. If I didn't eat something besides berries soon, my belly button would be touching my backbone.

Okay. So the gaff only works when the fish are close to the surface. Yeah, I'd learned that, twice now. But to not try was worse than trying and failing. But I couldn't just try the same stupid thing over and over.

You can't learn nothin' if you don't leave the yard.

I glanced upstream. There had to be another shallow spot up there. A spot to snag a salmon.

I climbed over the rocks and continued upstream. The brush was thicker. In a couple of spots I had to part it with my hands like I was swimming the breast-stroke. And everything was damp, and the water started working its way up my sleeves. I tried cinching my cuffs down on my raincoat, but the Velcro kept loosening up on its own.

And the creek was a narrow, deep channel. I just hoped it'd spread out again.

I heard a branch snap, and this time I didn't jump out of my boots or slam my head against any hard objects but just stopped and looked.

A wall of black fur disappeared into the brush in front of me. I stared at the spot. I wanted to keep going upstream. I had to eat, but didn't want to be eaten.

I kicked at the moss covering a log until it came free, then stomped on it. Then I saw movement on the other side of the creek, branches waving in the wind, but there was no breeze. More black fur, then a bear was at the edge of the creek. A small bear, a cub.

I took a step back.

The cub lapped some water from the creek, its nose resting on the surface. It was cute, made you want to sit down and play with it, but I knew it was a death trap. Mothers protected their cubs.

I turned around and picked my way downstream, glancing over my shoulder every couple of steps. Alert but calm, I thought. I didn't freak out and do something stupid. I was starting to really get this. If you didn't threaten something, or act like you were super nervous, then whatever else was around mellowed out too.

I broke out of the forest and walked along the stream bank through the beach grass, relieved to be out in the open. I'd rather starve than get attacked by a bear.

If I had to eat berries, I'd eat berries. I had to eat something. The more energy I spent looking for food, the hungrier I'd get. I'd just spent a few hours crawling up that creek and had nothing to show for it, except I'd learned that my gaff only worked if the fish were close to the surface and that being calm is a good thing. And yeah, I'd left the yard and learned I had to keep leaving the yard.

I didn't have time to learn things the slow way, the way Mom said she'd become a better guitar player and writer. Slow and steady. That was fine if you weren't trying to survive. Sure, I'd concentrate on gaffing a fish if I found some, but I couldn't spend weeks figuring out where they were.

The creek flared to the right and the beach grass grew taller—neck high. I took a breath and reminded myself to be alert but calm. I took another step and a faint rustling invaded my ears. Then I saw white, and more white, and some gray. And I relaxed and just stood there. And that was my first mistake. Not looking where I was going as I backed up was my second.

CHAPTER 14

A HISS like no other hiss I'd ever heard invaded my ears. Then this prehistoric beast was stretching its neck toward me, and flapping the biggest wings I'd ever seen. When I saw its bill was open and it wasn't stopping I took a couple big steps backward to avoid being pierced or bitten or whatever this thing was planning on doing. Behind it I glimpsed three or four more just like it, only more gray than white, before I went down.

Yeah, I caught my heel on something and landed flat on my back with my head in the creek. Two thumps on my chest and the monster swan was on top of me with its hissing bill descending toward my face. I turned and felt the water invade my mouth as my head went under, the swan's bill slicing my neck just below the ear. I came up choking, swinging my arms.

The swan danced back, still hissing. I spied the end of my gaff, scooped it up and kept advancing. All five of them turned and started flapping their wings through beach grass, eventually lifting off like jets with extremely heavy cargo.

I let out a breath, felt my heart pounding. My hand moved to my neck just below my ear and came back bloody. It stung like it had been blasted by a blowtorch. I'd just had my butt kicked by a bird. Yeah, it was a big bird. But still, it was a bird.

Okay, alert but calm doesn't work every time. And swans, they're tough. I'm just glad it hadn't connected with one of my eyes.

Mr. Haskins was always telling us weird animal stories but he didn't have any swan stories that I knew of.

I kept walking and broke out of the beach grass, I wiped more blood from my neck, forded the two side channels, the water pulling at my shins, then crossed the gravel bar. If I would've been thinking more clearly when that swan was on top of me I could've grabbed its neck and twisted. If I wanted to survive I needed to be ready to take advantage of any opportunity. If I'd been ready maybe I'd be cooking a big fat swan instead of wiping blood off my neck.

I approached the main channel of the creek and saw a splash. Like magic, a large school of fish filled the channel. I felt the power again; the whole place was humming. Only it wasn't a noise, it was more of a feeling. Like the fish were in charge. When they were here everyone noticed— the eagles, the gulls, the bears. Seals and sea lions ate salmon. And Killer Whales. Everything depended on them. Well, everything except for, maybe, killer-swans.

No fish earlier and now there were fish. I needed to figure this out.

Mom's lyrics rushed into my brain.

If you pay attention, you will know what the river knows.

I raised my gaff, brought it down hard, pulled a struggling fish from the school, then clubbed it with a rock.

I examined the gaff. The line had stretched, but just barely.

I waited. The fish returned, and I killed another. The gaff survived the second killing, but the lure was now half out of the barked-out area. I wanted more fish, but knew if I kept at it I'd lose my lure.

I cleaned the bigger of the two fish first. I took my knife, punched the tip into the opening just in front of the anal fin, and ran it up the belly, stopping just below the gills. I pulled the guts out and tossed them into the creek and let the gulls fight over them. Then I slit the bloodline, and, using my thumb while holding the fish in the water, I worked the blue-purple vein out of the fish, like my dad had taught me.

I cleaned the other fish, and paused for a moment when two bright pink egg sacs plopped out of the cavity. I knew people ate the eggs, but they looked pretty gross to me.

I tossed the eggs, along with the rest of the guts, into the creek, and rinsed my hands.

I had oil from the fish on my lips, cheeks and hands. I crunched the last of the burnt skin between my teeth. Then I sucked on the bones, trying to get every last bit of meat, but stopped short at the eyes. I couldn't take an eye out of a socket, or suck an eye out of a socket even though I knew they were packed with protein. Just the thought of it made my stomach lurch.

I threw the skeletons into the creek, and then took a long drink and splashed water on my face. I worked my hands into the sand and finely ground rock and scrubbed them like Dad had done to clean the dinner pot. I splashed some water on my raincoat and rain pants, hoping to rid them of the fish smell. Then I splashed water on my swan wound. I ran the tip of my finger along the slit in my skin, and it came back pink, coated with watery blood. And the area around the slit was sore, all the way from my earlobe to partway down my neck. I turned sideways, trying to see a reflection of it in the water but couldn't see anything. I splashed more water on it, hoping it wouldn't get infected.

I was about to head back to my kitchen when I spotted something way up the shoreline. A color that wasn't quite green just above the strand line in the trees. Almost blue, a waving blue. I'd see it and then I wouldn't. I'd see it and then I wouldn't. But one thing's for sure, I hadn't seen it when I'd walked the shoreline to get here a few days ago.

I jogged toward the disappearing and reappearing blue, keeping my eyes trained on the spot, my heart thumping through three layers of clothing, my swan bite throbbing.

It was more flung than hung. And the bottom six inches were shredded, like party confetti, or Christmas tree tinsel, but the rest of it was intact.

I reached out and pulled it from the branches. One of the sleeves caught but another tug freed it. Now it was in my hands. My throat tightened up and I swallowed.

"Dad?" I said, the word barely moving beyond my lips.

I took a breath, let it out and then inhaled. Then I yelled, "Dad! Dad, Dad, Dad!"

It was his raincoat.

Back at my kitchen, I scooped some live coals out of the fire ring with a thick piece of bark, then went to my sleep shelter and got the fires going. I'd searched and searched, and called and called. And I'd scanned the forest floor and thin strip of beach around the raincoat for footprints but all I'd found were bear tracks. Maybe the jacket washed ashore and a bear had picked it up? Was my dad wearing that jacket when the boat flipped? I couldn't remember. I knew he at least had it in his cockpit. And I knew it was raining but maybe he hadn't had time to put his jacket on. I had my jacket on from the start because I was cold but my dad never wore his unless it was raining.

If he's around, he has to see the smoke from my fire, or at least smell it. But if he's hurt, he might not be able to walk. But I hadn't seen any tracks by the jacket, but maybe the tide had erased his tracks? Maybe it means he's coming? Maybe it's a sign, telling me to hang on because he's coming. Maybe he's walking the shoreline of Hidden Bay right now like I had a couple days ago.

Tomorrow I'd make this shelter better. More home-like. And warmer. And I'd build a shelter for the kitchen. I'd build it big enough for two.

I'm moving in, I thought. Where the fish are. Where the power is. Where my dad's coming to.

Then it hit me. Exploded in my mind like fireworks. The tide. The fish run with the incoming tide. Fishing is always better on an incoming tide, that's what Dad had said. The tide must help the salmon upstream. Push them upstream.

I'd have to tune in to the tides if I wanted to catch fish. And if I didn't catch fish . . . I'd be the food.

BEFORE THE ACCIDENT

Three-foot seas with a little chop on top were washing over the bow of the kayak. Doesn't sound big but it's no joke when you're sitting at the water line. You have to keep moving or else you'll be tossed around by the waves.

The east side of Bear Island—no man's land, Dad called it. Not that we'd seen many people anywhere since we'd hit the water a couple weeks ago.

I set my paddle across the combing of the cockpit, pulled my spray skirt up and cinched it tight around my chest with the toggle. The nylon skirt stretched around the combing, sealing me in. It was supposed to keep any water out that splashed over the boat.

I kept digging my paddle into the water. Home. Home. Home, I said to myself. Every paddle-stroke was one step closer. But the head wind and approaching waves slowed us down. Like paddling through molasses instead of water.

We rounded another point and hit bigger water. The kayak shook side to side when the waves passed under the boat. Every third or fourth wave buried the tip of the kayak but then it'd bounce back, riding on top. Dad steered us around some sea stacks, carrying us farther from shore.

Then the clouds started spitting rain. I put my hood up but the wind blew it off.

CHAPTER 15

THE NEXT morning I walked to the bay. Not right to the mouth of the stream, but down a ways. Dad said it was better for everything to just go into the ocean instead of the woods. I thought it was kind of odd but figured he knew more about it than I did. Before the accident we'd used toilet paper which we put in a baggie and then burned when we had a fire, but Dad told me once he'd run out of TP on a solo trip and used salt water.

Yeah, it was kind of gross, but clean at the same time. I had an unlimited supply of water, but sometimes had to use my hands a little more than I would've liked. I'd wash them off, scrub them with gravel, and then give them the sniff test. And if they smelled like crap, I'd wash them until they didn't.

You always hear about people using moss. I tried that, but moss just breaks apart and sticks to you in a place you don't want it to stick. And sometimes it's full of dirt or has a bunch of spruce needles in it, or tiny spiders. And that's the last place I'd want spiders crawling around.

The clouds were piling up to the south. The tide was way out—the stream channels just a series of dark slivers cutting through the seaweed. No chance of gaffing a fish for hours. I'd just have to survive on berries until the tide turned. But I had other things to do, too.

Collect wood.

Fix gaff.

Build kitchen shelter.

Fix up bedroom.

"Bedroom?" I shook my head as I turned from the water. "Yeah. Bedroom. I mean, it doesn't have a bed, but it's where I bed down. And it's a type of room. Bedroom."

I pictured my room at home, with the dark blue drapes to keep the summer sun out so I could sleep, and heavy to keep the heat from escaping in the winter. Would I ever sleep there again? I spent a lot of time in there after Mom died. When my dad wasn't sleeping he would just sit at the kitchen table or in the living room, and he'd talk like he was just learning. One-word answers, and he wouldn't talk unless I talked to him first.

And for that whole first year I thought if Mom was gone I may as well be gone, too. Like I was part of a package deal and now the deal was off. And I thought Dad blamed me for Mom's death too. I mean, he never told me he did, but he never told me he didn't. Never. And he was right there when she asked me if I wanted to go on the ride and I chose to practice with my bow instead. The last thing she'd said was: "If you're not going, I'm gonna bike the whole loop." And later that month my dad burned my bow and target.

For a while I let my mom's guitar gather dust in the living room just like everything else in the house. One day I picked it up and took it to my room. The first time I strummed it, Dad opened my bedroom door and just stared at me with this pained look on his face. His eyes teared up and he turned and walked out. After that I played softly and I'd stuff a blanket in the crack between the door and floor to keep the sound from traveling. I didn't want to cause my dad any more pain, but I wanted to stay connected to my mom. I had to play her guitar. And sing her songs. It was my way of talking to her. Seeing her. Being with her.

I stoked one of the fires, then hauled armloads of firewood back to my bedroom. When I found berries I ate them. The juices stung the wounds in my mouth. Instead of healing, they'd turned into large canker sores. And every time I poked at them with my tongue, they burned. I couldn't help poking them. I was continually checking to see if they were gone, and they never were. And a steady ache had settled in around the swan bite, like maybe it was infected. When I touched the area around the bite it felt bumpy, like a rash. And it was starting to itch.

I lugged some deadfall to the kitchen area. I think they were a bunch of small trees that were mowed down in a snow avalanche or a windstorm, because they'd all fallen in the same direction, like a giant had walked down the mountain, flattening everything in its path.

And all the time I scavenged for wood and berries I kept my eyes and ears open for any sign of my dad. I'd found some broken plastic bottles in the strand line and a rusty fishing lure without any hooks, but that was it.

My back muscles just below my shoulders ached every time I pulled on anything, but I just kept on pulling because that's how you dealt with deadfall. You grabbed an end and pulled. Sometimes it came with you straight away, and other times you had to lift with one hand and pull with the other, or pull with both arms and lean backwards, or change your angle. Sometimes it broke free and you fell backwards or sideways.

But you had to pull.

Pull.

Pull.

Pull.

I leaned five long poles against a large spruce, at forty-five degree angles, and spaced about a foot apart.

I carried rocks from the shore and piled them around the base of each pole. Then collected branches and laid them lengthwise across the poles. All I wanted was a place to cook and eat where I wouldn't get pounded by the rain. A place far enough away from my bedroom so any bears that checked out my kitchen wouldn't stumble into my bedroom. A place big enough for me and my dad.

I broke boughs from spruce and hemlock trees and covered part of the bedroom floor, big enough for two to sleep. They'd keep us off the moss and mud, and smelled good, kind of like oranges. I wanted to pile more in—make a bed of them that was really raised off the ground, and cover the kitchen floor too, but then I remembered the tide.

I ran to the creek. The salt water was pushing its way upstream. And a thick mat of dorsal fins rode in the tide.

I felt the digestive juices building at the bottom of my esophagus, burning.

I jogged back to my bedroom, put a piece of wood on the fire and grabbed my gaff.

The gaff.

I hadn't fixed it yet.

It didn't matter if I worked all day and half the night, there was always more to do.

I pulled on the loose hook. The rope that ran through all the fishing line had somehow stretched. After picking away at the knot and being unsuccessful, I just cut the rope, repositioned the lure, and retied the rope.

I'd have to think of a better way tonight. I couldn't afford to lose another lure, but I couldn't afford to not fish while the tide was in.

───

That night, two burncooked fish filled out my stomach as I sat between the fires in my bedroom.

And in my hands, a hookless gaff.

That rope I'd retied, the line sliced right through it when I'd hooked my third fish.

I was a bear without claws. And as Mr. Haskins put it: "You know what happens in nature when you don't adapt? You die."

A single salmon laid hundreds of eggs. And it got to lay those eggs only after avoiding all those animals in the ocean that might eat them and fishermen that might catch them, and then dodging bears in the creek. Some made it, some didn't. And the ones that made it passed their genes on so those fish created from the eggs were more likely to make it, unless the conditions changed.

And people who survived in tough situations didn't make the same mistakes over and over. They adapted or else they died.

Like this dude, Shackelton. I'd read a book about him and his men stranded on the frozen Antarctic Ocean a hundred years ago, their ship crushed by sea ice. Cut off from the world, they hiked hundreds of miles over the shifting ice pack, constantly changing what they were doing to adapt to their constantly changing situation. None of them had died. They hauled these big wooden boats, weighing hundreds of pounds, over the ice. It was backbreaking work. Some of the men wanted to abandon the boats, but Shackelton said no because they might reach a point where they'd need them. He kept his options open—those boats saved their lives.

I knew I needed to fix the gaff, had to make it better. But I needed something else, in case I kept losing hooks. Another option.

Something that didn't rely on a hook.

Learning life's lessons sure can be hard.

You can't learn nothin' if you don't leave the yard.

I tossed the gaff aside and picked up a branch about seven feet long that I'd broken from an alder tree, and started whittling. The alder was stubborn and my knife kept skipping forward. And my eyes kept wanting to close.

Just 'cause a job looks big, especially when you're tired, doesn't mean you can't do it. You can't let your own mind talk you out of it before you even try.

"One shaving at a time," I told myself over and over.

I whittled and whittled, taking short breaks to stretch my fingers and wrists, and to add wood to the fires. I'd named them Right Fire (RF) and Left Fire (LF).

LF gave me problems. That little devil was always blowing smoke into my eyes. He ate more wood because of the wind fanning him. But that wind made LF hotter than RF, so he kept me warmer.

RF was a steady burner, mostly thanks to me acting as a wind block. I usually turned to RF in the morning. He always had hot coals, unless the wind had switched.

"I'd have hot coals too," LF said. "If you'd give me my fair share of wood."

"Fair share?" I said. "Dude, you burn everything like it's been doused in gas."

Yeah, they talked to me and I talked to them. I mean, who else was I going to talk to? I fed them wood and they fed me warmth. I'd do my best to make sure they didn't die, and whether they knew it or not, they were doing the same for me. I knew a bear could tear through the front wall of my shelter, but the fires might make a bear hesitate, or stay away. And being able to see when it was dark made things less scary. I could feel the nights getting longer and longer, and I couldn't afford to just sleep when it got dark 'cause I needed the time to work.

The part of my thumb facing my index finger blistered from gripping the knife, but I just kept whittling until the last eight inches or so of the branch tapered to a point.

I felt the point with my finger. "It should puncture."

"Not bad," RF said, "for your first time."

"Puncture?" LF said. "Looks kind of dull."

"What
do you two
know?" I said.
"Sharpness is one
thing. Force is another."
Like me and Billy—with
our arrows back in fifth grade.
They weren't that sharp, but when we
put our weight behind them they stuck.
Billy used to come over after school to shoot at
the target my dad had set up in the backyard. Then my mom died and that
was the end of that.

Billy was a good shot. Said there was nothing to it—he just imagined
the target was his dad. I wondered how Billy would feel if his dad actually
died. Would Billy miss him? It'd be hard to miss someone who made a
habit of hitting you.

My dad had never hit me with anything except his silence. The most
violent he ever got was breaking all those dishes after Mom died.

My dad, I thought.

"What do you think," I said to LF, leaning toward him. "Is he around?"

LF belched a cloud of smoke into my eyes and I drew back. "Okay, so
that's how it's gonna be." I turned to RF. "What do you think? Is my dad
around here? Is...is he even alive?"

RF continued to burn steadily, then it popped and an orange flame
crawled over the top stick and the fire flared.

"Cool," I said. "I'll take that as a *yes*."

I set the spear down, held my hands in front of LF and rubbed them
together. Wishing hadn't brought Mom back and I knew that technically
it wouldn't magically bring Dad to me, but still, that raincoat, that had to

be a sign. The life vest, too. And the footprints. And all the times I'd heard his voice.

Nice spear, Tom. Now, what about that gaff?

I smiled and then picked up the gaff. Should I put another lure on it? No, I thought. I have to make the gaff better so I don't lose any more lures.

In my mind I worked at fixing the gaff, trying to see a better way. A stronger way.

I put another log on LF, some smaller sticks on RF.

RF immediately popped and threw sparks.

"Okay, okay," I said. "I'll give you a log too." I put a log on RF. "You happy, now?"

RF smoked a bit, and then popped.

I removed lure number three from my survival kit.

I tied another five independent loops of fishing line through the eyehole, and was reaching for the rope when I heard the noise.

CHAPTER 16

NEEDLES crunched. I heard a shuffle, then a grunt. My heart beat in my ears, like my head was gonna explode.

Something bumped my shelter. I pressed my back against the dirt wall. A small branch moved.

The branch detached itself from my shelter.

I screamed, "Hey bear! Hey bear! Hey bear!"

But nothing happened. I felt the sweat building under my arms. My whole body was shaking. I took a breath and a chill ran up my spine.

Seconds passed. I heard it. A chewing, gnawing sound filled my ears and became my whole world.

Not a big sound. A small sound. I cupped my hands behind my ears and listened. I turned my head toward one entrance then the other, trying to pinpoint the location. Just beyond the light of LF. That's where I thought it was coming from.

I stood, and the sound stopped. But I could sense that whatever made the sound was close by, covered only by the darkness.

I grabbed the unburnt end of a log I'd been feeding to LF, who responded by blowing a stream of gray smoke my way. Then I put the glowing end forward, and stepped outside. But the red glow was so dim I could barely see my own feet.

Back inside, I knelt and piled handfuls of small sticks on both LF and RF, filling the shelter with warmth and light.

I thought about just staying put, but I had to see what was out there. Had to know if it was something to worry about.

I stood again, flush with the back of the shelter, and was about to step outside, but stopped. I reached toward the boughs and scooped up my new spear. I tapped the tip with my index finger. Sharp enough.

I took a breath and stepped into the added light, and peered in the direction where I'd heard the gnawing, chewing noises. Under a tree, less than twenty feet away, was a curled-up form twice the size of a football, the tips of its quills shining in the firelight.

I felt my hand tighten around the base of the spear.

A porcupine.

Food. Meat. Food. Meat.

Every starving cell in my skinny body was sending signals to my brain. Kill it. Eat it. Kill it. Eat it.

On the tips of my toes I took a step toward the porcupine.

No response.

I took another step. Then another.

When I'd covered half the distance, the porcupine turned its head away from me and presented its tail.

Careful, I thought.

Only about eight feet away, I gripped the base of the spear with both hands and brought it up to ear-level. I took two quick steps, and lunged forward. The porcupine swung its tail in my direction. I felt the spear point connect, and kept driving it forward into its neck.

The porcupine thrashed wildly, wailed like a baby, and ripped the spear from my hands. The spear bounced up and down until I pinned it to the ground with my feet. And through my boot bottoms I could feel the spear shaking, the little animal quivering. It went on for maybe ten or fifteen seconds, the life draining out of it. Then nothing.

I stepped off the spear and grabbed it with both hands. I was pretty sure the porcupine was dead, but I drove the spear forward and down, listening and feeling for movement. One stray swat with that tail and I'd be hurting.

I lifted the spear, heavy with death, with food. Still, I kept it fully extended. I'd seen salmon that I'd pummeled spring back to life.

At the band of alders in front of my bedroom I wove the spear between the branches, suspending the porcupine off the ground.

In the dim light I saw the porcupine's open mouth, like it was still crying out in agony. I cringed and looked away. I felt bad for killing it, but satisfied, too.

It felt different than pulling a fish from the creek—there were thousands of salmon swimming up this one stream, but there weren't thousands of porcupines running around. I'd only seen this one the whole time. But if I saw another, I'd try to kill it, too.

Things died all the time so other things could live. Animals searched for plants and other animals to eat while they tried not to get eaten.

Death is part of life. Part of the cycle. No one escapes it.

Just last year a bunch of wolves had killed this woman who was jogging down a dirt road outside a remote village. I felt bad for the woman and everyone who knew her and everyone who would miss her and at the same time knew that those wolves were just being wolves, killing to eat, like animals did.

I looked at the porcupine again. So small, and I'd killed it. And that high-pitched sound, like a baby crying when the spear connected. I thought about my own neck, how horrible it'd be to get stabbed with a spear, but I needed to eat, just like the wolves.

I decided to wait until morning to gut it, clean it, cook it and eat it. In the light. In the kitchen.

I added wood to LF and RF and lay down on the life vests. The canker sores in my mouth ached, and my swan bite itched like a hundred mosquitos had nailed me right on that spot, but I was smiling.

———

In the morning by the fire in my kitchen, I studied the speared porcupine. Couldn't be much different from gutting a fish. Just slit open the belly and pull the insides out.

With my foot I pushed the porcupine off the spear and turned it over, belly upwards. I slit the soft quill-less belly, reached into the opening and pulled out the guts, which felt like a giant handful of jello coated with glue, and smelled like cat food. Gross.

I carried the guts to the bay, tossed them in, then stuck my hands in the water and rubbed them together. I pulled them out and shook them, then did the sniff test. They still smelled like cat-food so I scrubbed them more, this time with gravel.

Back in the kitchen, I tried to cut into the animal but the quills kept getting in the way, poking me.

I'd never heard of anyone eating a porcupine. Do you have to skin it? Too hard to skin with all those quills. Maybe I could just singe those suckers off?

I jabbed the spear through the open belly and into its throat, then rolled the carcass over the fire, letting the flames burn the quills down to tiny nubs. I pulled it from the fire and scraped off the nubs with my knife. And that charred-skin smell sent my stomach dancing.

After the fire burned down, I put some green alder on the coals and set the carcass on the alder. While it cooked, I gathered some firewood and got a drink from the creek.

When it started to turn black, I knocked it off the fire and let it cool until I could pick it up without being burned.

I gnawed on the ribs, ripping meat from the bones and then chewing. The porcupine meat proved to be as tough as fish was tender. Instead of easily falling off the bones like the salmon, it clung to them.

So I chewed and chewed and chewed.

And then I chewed some more.

My jaw got tired. It tightened up. But I kept at it, ripping into the tough-as-leather meat, swallowing mouthful after mouthful.

I picked the ribs and back clean, and then hung the carcass in a tree, saving the legs for later. I glanced at the carcass and thought, "later?" Yeah, it was only one more meal. I could actually work on my shelters and not worry about going hungry, at least for today.

> Porcupine by my shelter, its armor all intact.
> I was starving so I stabbed it, and it tried to stab me back.
> All its quills were quivering, as its life drained from its neck.
> I was sad and was happy. I'd eat it, every speck.

My mom could've put my words to music. If I actually got to take guitar lessons I'd give it a try, if I could remember the words. The Salmon Song, the Porcupine Song—if I'd made more I'd already forgotten them.

I piled spruce boughs on my bedroom roof until it was a dark green mound pushing out from the bank. The fog rolled in as I carried rocks up the beach and lined the base where the roof met the ground both inside and out, and dumped handfuls of beach gravel on top of the rocks to fill in the cracks to keep out the cold.

And I thought about the creek full of salmon. I couldn't turn my back on that. Maybe someone would come poking around back here. I mean, my dad couldn't be the only one who wanted to get into the wilderness. Maybe I wouldn't even have to go to the Sentinels.

BEFORE THE ACCIDENT

"Bigger water out there," Dad shouted. "Need a place to land. Maybe around the next point. Just keep paddling. Hard. We want to avoid that wind line."

I bent forward and dug my paddle deeper, in a race against the dark gray water marching toward us. We'd been overtaken by a couple of wind lines, but they'd been no big deal. Just turned flat water into one- and two-foot seas. But the waves were already four feet and breaking.

CHAPTER 17

TWELVE DAYS later, and I'd worn a trail between my bedroom and kitchen. And with the help of RF and LF, we'd come up with a name. Fish Camp. It made sense to me because I wouldn't be here if it weren't for the fish. And we all agreed that it sounded nicer than Swan-bite Camp. Yeah, that thing still itched some but it was getting better.

After the porcupine, I'd started keeping track of the days. I don't even know why. I guess I just wanted to know, so every day I scratched a line on my spear with my knife. I counted backwards and figured it'd been about eleven days between the accident and the porcupine, so I put eleven more marks on the spear. Twenty-three total. Since the raincoat, I hadn't received any more signs that my dad was close by, even though I was always looking, always hoping.

I didn't know what else to do besides live at Fish Camp. You'd think I'd go crazy from loneliness, but I had almost no time to be lonely, except at night. And usually I was so tired I just drifted in and out of sleep, making sure to keep RF and LF going. Some nights I'd wake up in a sweat, reliving the accident. Then I'd really build up the fires and lay there in the light, the weight of my mistake pressing down on me.

Sometimes I'd think about Heather and whether she was really moving back to Fairbanks. Would I ever get back to see her? And if I did make it back but my dad didn't, would I get to stay in Fairbanks, or would I have to go live with my uncle who I barely knew?

And I'd think about my mom and that bike ride, and I'd go back and forth on whether it was my fault. And even if it wasn't my fault, I still felt bad about how things would've been different if I'd gone on the ride. How we would've still been a family instead of two people barely speaking to each other living in the same house.

Most nights I woke up thirsty but didn't want to walk to the creek in the dark.

I'd tacked up one of the silver emergency blankets on the dirt wall. It reflected both warmth and light from RF and LF.

I'd cut a piece of nylon from the shredded end of my dad's raincoat and wrapped it around the rope on my gaff. That kept the fishing line from cutting through it.

And yesterday I learned by accident that I could dry fish. A bear had come into my camp. I had three fish on the fire, almost done. The bear came toward me, attracted by the fish smell, and then retreated as I waved my spear and shouted. This went on for a long time, until I started throwing rocks. No one ever told me to throw rocks at a bear. It was always "play dead, yell or speak softly, back away slowly, or hold your ground or make yourself look big." All these contradictions. But after I pegged the small bear a couple of times it drew back, then disappeared.

When I turned to the fire, the bottom sides of the fish were so burned they were crispy around the tail and had started to dry out. I wasn't sure how long dried, burned fish would keep, but knew it was my ticket out.

The salmon in the stream were thinning out. Fewer fish in the school each day. And Fish Camp would be useless without the salmon. I was at the very back of a big bay on the exposed side of Bear Island, a place I remembered Dad saying that people stayed away from. Too far and too expensive. And now it was fall, no one was gonna be paddling out here. In the back of my mind I still hoped someone would show up, but I couldn't count on it.

But deciding to strike out from Fish Camp was still a mixed bag. I'd grown used to sleeping in the same place between the warmth and protection of LF and RF. And the fish had made the difference between life and death. I was thinner than I'd ever been, but I think I'd stopped losing weight since I'd been eating two or three salmon every day.

I'd staked out my territory and was living in it. I'd chased that bear off. And I'd found Dad's raincoat here. And Fish Camp was closer to where the accident happened. Closer to where I'd last seen my dad.

Still, I knew that my chance of survival depended on my leaving. I could slowly starve to death in my comfortable camp, or I could continue my journey to the Sentinels, where I hoped to spot a boat or run into some hunters. And, it'd be where my dad would go. Maybe the waves carried him across the mouth of Hidden Bay and he'd searched for me for a while and then headed to the Sentinels. It was possible. By water, the mouth of Hidden Bay and the site of the accident weren't that far apart. And if anyone could survive some extended time in the water, it was my dad. But even if one or both of us made it to the Sentinels that didn't ensure anything.

If only someone had known that we were going to Bear Island, to the Sentinels, or if Dad hadn't hid the truck in Whittier. Then getting rescued wouldn't feel like such a long shot.

CHAPTER 18

I HAD the dead fish by the tail, and was about to slit the belly when I saw the alders waving. I dropped the fish next to the other four I'd gaffed, and stood up.

"Dad," I yelled. "Dad?"

Just across the creek, a black bear emerged from the forest.

I thought about tossing a fish across the creek as a peace offering, but I needed these fish. All of them.

The bear stood on its hind legs, wagged its head back and forth. My knife, with its four-inch blade, felt tiny in my hand.

My body was shaking. This bear was twice as big as the one I'd chased out of my camp.

Don't run, don't run, don't run, I told myself.

I bent, picked up my gaff, and held it over my head.

The bear took another few steps toward me.

I wished I were in camp. In my territory.

"Hey bear! Hey bear! Hey bear!"

The bear dropped from its hind legs and came forward again, like I was calling it over.

I sucked in a breath. Maybe I should just shut up. Or pick up a rock and throw it. I wished there was fire between me and that bear instead of water.

Now it stood at the edge of the channel. Like thirty feet away. The tan spots standing out on either side of its snout. And its head was tilted, the way Billy's dog would tilt hers when I whistled.

I still had the gaff raised. If it came after me, I'd do what I could. Take a swing at it. Try to drive it away. Use my knife if it was on top of me.

Then the bear lay down, kicked all four legs up and moved side to side, scratching its back on the rocks. Then it rolled to one side, rose on four legs and disappeared upstream without looking back.

Luck, just luck. I knew I couldn't be lucky forever.

I worked all day and all night and all the next day, drying my fish.

I hauled rocks from the beach and built a pad so I could take fish off the fire without rolling them in the dirt. I found two small sturdy spruce trees growing close together, and used these to break alder for my supply of grill-wood by positioning long pieces between the trees and pulling until the alder broke.

I'd let the fish cook on the grill until the tail turned crispy. With sticks, I'd roll the fish onto the rock pad and replace any of the alder that had burnt up.

After each fish cooled enough so I could touch it, I cut the head off. Then I'd peel the top half of the fish from the bones, set it aside and remove the backbone and ribs attached to the bottom half. If the fish was cooked, then the bones slid right out.

Then I put both halves back on the alder grill, and let them cook until they were crispy.

I gnawed on the fish heads, eating the skin and the little bits of meat. And, for the first time, I ate the eyes of the fish, knowing I'd need every ounce of energy I could find.

I thought Dad would be proud of how I'd taken his method for cooking salmon and made it work for drying fish.

I dried five fish, but was dead tired.

Dad's rule about no food in the tent made sense when you could hang your food up high on a rope, and you had a kayak to travel in. But this food, it was my life. Even if it did attract bears, I just had to have it with me while I slept.

That night, in my bedroom, I did what I usually did. I pulled my boots off and tipped them sideways in front of LF, peeled my damp socks from my feet and spread them out on some boughs close to RF.

The worst thing about taking my feet out of my boots was the smell. My feet reeked like boiled cabbage. And since I hadn't been out of my boots for two days 'cause of the round-the-clock fish drying, they stunk worse than usual. But I had bigger problems than that.

I pulled out my survival kit. The two Meal Pack Bars stared at me, and I felt a lump in my throat. I set them aside and focused on the real problem.

One of the lighters had stopped working.

I counted fifteen matches.

I pulled out the flint. My dad had shown me how to use it. I didn't know if it was true flint, but that's what he called it. It was silver, about an inch long cylinder as thin as a pencil, attached to a tiny plastic handle. In the winter, in the wall tent, sometimes, I'd play with it. It was pretty easy to get a spark but to turn that spark into fire—that was the trick.

I opened my knife and ran the blade across the flint, causing a large spark to form, fall and disappear.

The spark's got to hit some very small, dry flammable material—like dried grass or wood shavings or tiny scraps of birch bark. And then, you've got to blow on it and feed it.

I wished Dad would've put another lighter in each kit. And more matches. That's what he should've done.

My chest tightened. If the lighter stopped working and I ran out of matches, the flint would be my only hope.

And what if I couldn't do it? What if I could do everything else, but this one lousy thing I failed at? Then what?

I needed more matches and lighters, not stupid flint or idiot Meal Pack Bars.

Fire. Fire. Fire.

Didn't Dad know how important it would be?

I still hoped someone would just show up before I even set off to the Sentinels.

But if no one came, I'd have to build my fire from scratch every night.

I ran the blade across the flint again, and watched another spark disappear into the boughs. Could you really start a fire with a spark in a wet place like this? I doubted it. I hoped the lighter would last.

But if I hadn't found his vest I'd have less. A lot less.

I might not even be alive if I hadn't found his vest.

And he'd taught me so much. And wherever he was, because of his voice, I was still learning from him.

Gaffing the five fish today had taken every ounce of my concentration and experience. The run had thinned out. And I'd noticed more and more carcasses of spawned-out salmon the last few days, some floating on top of the water, and others bouncing along the stream bottom, driven by the current.

I didn't want to end up like those fish. And I thought, if I died out here, it'd be worse. Those salmon had already lived most of their lives. Dying after spawning was what was supposed to happen. Their bodies were programmed to croak. If I died, I'd be missing out on the rest of my life, just like my mom.

But if I died, I wouldn't be around to miss anything. And when I thought of death this way, it didn't seem as scary.

What scared me more was what it would feel like to be dying if I starved to death, or froze to death, or was attacked by a bear. Or if I was so weak that the gulls pecked my eyes out while I was alive.

Nothing would change on Bear Island if I died. The fish would still spawn. The bears would still catch them. The eagles and gulls and porcupines would still scavenge. The trees would still grow. The tide would rise and fall.

I wouldn't be missed. I was a small part of a big place. But at least at this place, this one creek, I felt like I belonged.

———

The next day I converted my dad's raincoat into a fanny pack to carry the fish. I tied the fish together with a piece of rope, and then rolled them up in my dad's raincoat, and used two pieces of rope to secure the coat around the fish. I tied the coat around my waist with the arms.

I threaded the two life vests through the fish-fanny-pack jacket so they hung behind me,

Before I left, I walked over to my kitchen shelter and took one last look. I'd left nothing except the word 'sentinels' made from rocks I'd hauled up the beach, in case my dad was still working his way south and was behind me.

The sun broke free from behind the clouds and blasted my eyes as I crossed the creek and worked my way along the rocky shore. The tide was out. I heard blows, put my hand to my forehead to make a visor, scanned the water, and counted. Six Killer Whales—a family—milling in the bay, their white cheek patches just visible above the water line. Black curved fins rising from rounded backs. Two of them were much smaller, like half the size, of the bigger ones.

"Killer Whales stay together for life," my dad had told me. "You're born into a family and you stay in that family. You're never alone."

With the smaller whales in the middle of the pack, I watched them swim along the opposite shore and then disappear around a point. "A family," I whispered. "A real family."

I kept walking and started to sweat, so I took off my raincoat and tied it around my waist.

Little fish darted in and out of the protection of rocks and seaweed as I splashed through the intertidal zone. Islands of black mussels clinging to rocky, muddy sludge dotted the ground.

Eating shellfish on a trip is risky business. They can have bacteria that can kill you, especially if there's a red tide. Don't know much about when it's okay to eat them. Wish I did because they sure are good.

Oh Dad. How do you know all this stuff? The exact stuff that I need to know. How?

When I'd first washed ashore and heard his voice about the survival kit, it'd startled me. But now, the voice was more like a friend, like it didn't matter if it was coming from somewhere outside me or from within me. What mattered was that I could hear it.

Maybe it was him, my family, pulling me to the Sentinels because he was there.

I turned and saw my shadow stretching toward Fish Camp. I could see where my stream entered the bay, where my home had been. A tiny lump formed in the back of my throat and I swallowed it down.

Part of me wanted to go back and just stay. It would be easier than what I was doing now. But I knew that choosing the easy path meant choosing death. And I wanted to live.

BEFORE THE ACCIDENT

I picked up the pace some more and tried to match my dad stroke for stroke. The outside of my forearms started to burn. Sweat ran down my neck.

Dig, dig, dig, I told myself. Just keep digging.

We quartered the first set of six-foot waves, no problem. Dad had a good angle; that's one key to keeping your boat stable in big seas. The other thing you need to do is keep your speed up.

So I kept digging my paddle in, pulling hard and fast, but it felt like we were standing still. The boat rocked once and I barely caught the top of a wave with my paddle. My back slammed against the seat.

"Paddle harder if you can!" I knew my dad had shouted that, but his voice sounded far away because of the headwind.

The waves were bouncing off the coast back into the passage, rocking us both sideways and back and forth. I just kept digging in. We could do it. We just needed to keep moving, or find a protected place to stake out.

CHAPTER 19

TWO DAYS later, clouds covered the sky, but still, it didn't rain. Wind screamed up the cliffs, rattling my raincoat, as I worked my way along a forested bluff a few hundred feet above the bay. I'd eaten a fish and a half each in the last two days, leaving me with just two fish, and I wasn't even out of Hidden Bay.

The leaves of the blueberry plants blazed deep red, a few shriveled berries clinging to the branches. The deer cabbage turned the muskegs into blankets of red and yellow with little bits of green mixed in. And the mountain peaks were dusted with fresh snow.

I could see why my dad and mom loved this place, even though I mostly hated it now. Could you hate something this beautiful? I hated it and I loved it. If I could just eat the beauty, I'd never go hungry. But you can't eat beauty, and it seems I was always hungry.

Every step had been hard-earned yesterday as I picked my way along a jagged coast bordered by thick forest. My spear and gaff snagged in brush and smacked against small trees that grew so close together I had to turn sideways to pass between some of them.

I spent the last couple of nights by big fires without a shelter, but with these dark clouds, I'd have to build one tonight, and that would take time. I could feel the moist air, taste it. Just a matter of time before the clouds opened up and started dumping.

I kept moving through the trees, then up ahead I saw open space.

The forest was giving way to a gently sloping, treeless land that stretched from just above the water's edge to the base of the mountains.

I took a breath and smiled. Looked like some easy walking ahead.

Slabs of gray rock—some as big as football fields—separated by mats of low growing vegetation, stretched out before me. Miniature bluffs, ten feet high, with tiny valleys beneath them, dotted the slope. Moisture collected in the valleys creating little muskegs, while the bluff areas were dry tundra.

I'd taken a few steps onto the tundra when I spied the berries. Little black berries.

"Crowberries," I remembered.

Mom had shown me these berries the summer she died. We'd driven to the top of Murphy Dome, a place above tree line, to pick blueberries, but I'd seen the crowberries, too. You could eat them; I remembered that. And that they didn't taste like much of anything.

I dropped my spear and gaff, knelt with my back to the wind and gorged on the seedy berries. More of my mom's lyrics invaded my brain.

> *Food for the stomach and food for the soul.*
> *The land will feed you until you're still.*
> *Let your body sink into the ground.*
> *Feed it what you've got and it'll come back around.*

One thing Mom liked about Fairbanks, the town was an island surrounded by an empty sea of forested hills and tundra. She said the landscape fueled her stories and songs. And she wrote and wrote until the very last day of her life. In her stories, she was always sending some girl out into the woods with almost nothing. Her characters ate crowberries, insects, voles, and chewed on willow bark. But her characters always survived, except for one. And I remember Dad saying something like, "Yeah, it's sad that she died, but it's realistic."

I stuffed more berries into my mouth and wondered if anyone had found the truck in Whittier, and if searchers had already been to the Sentinels.

Had any of our gear been found? It could've drifted for miles. Pushed back and forth with the tides, or washed up on shore and then covered with seaweed or stuck in the rocks in places no one could get to, like the blue dry bag I'd seen. The more I thought about this, the more convinced I became that no one would find me.

Dad's face, bobbing in the waves popped into my mind. He was alive the last time I'd seen him. Still, my own death lurked in the back of my brain, waiting for me to make a fatal mistake, or just give up. And what would I do if I survived and my dad didn't? What difference would it make? I'd be an orphan. An orphan. I felt my face getting hot. I squeezed my eyes closed a couple of times, opened them and then kept going.

I hadn't heard Dad's voice in a while, except for last night when I woke with a gasp, the cold waves pushing me under. Only in this dream I couldn't make it to the surface. And through the water I looked up and saw my dad floating face down, waving at me. And I just kept sinking until I couldn't see him.

I had bad dreams after Mom's accident, but they were about what was happening to her, not me.

I stuck to the small bluffs, where the walking was easier. But my feet ached from walking all day in the rubber boots. I could feel the blisters forming on the insides of my arches and on the tops of my toes, hot spots burning with every step.

I heard the water before I saw it. A constant roar.

At the edge of a gorge, I looked toward the bay and then upstream, toward the snowy mountains. On the far side of the gorge the open land continued a little longer and then turned into forest; that's where I needed to be.

I walked along the rim of the gorge downstream, searching for a place to cross, but was soon staring over the tops of trees on a steep slope next to a huge waterfall. The white water rushed over the lip and plunged maybe sixty feet, the mist continually floating up, covering my face. It was Lord-of-the-Rings beautiful, but I hated it. All I wanted was a muddy trickle that I could step across.

I turned and headed upstream.

With the wind at my back, I climbed up and over little hills of jagged rocks. Then I saw two lakes in the distance, surrounded by forest and connected by a channel.

The first lake was small, a holding pond for the stream that rushed down the gorge. The water was shallow and spread out and had a current. While the water was still wide and shallow, I crossed the stream just below the little lake, and hiked the shore toward the larger lake.

The big lake filled most of the valley. At the far end a forested pass led to . . . somewhere.

I felt the breeze on my face as I stared at the pass. Was it a shortcut to the Sentinels? I didn't know. If only I had a map. What if I went that way and ran into cliffs on the other side of the pass? I put my tongue where the canker sores had been, and felt two bumps where scar tissue had grown.

The first drops of rain splashed on the lake. I turned to a twisted spruce tree, broke dead twigs from the low branches, and stuffed them into my pocket.

I couldn't just stand here and freeze. One more day, and maybe I'd be on the open coast. And maybe I'd spot a boat. No chance of that if I headed inland.

Two more bays between Hidden Bay and the Sentinels, or three? And how many miles of open coast? I couldn't remember.

A shortcut would be sweet.

I took a couple steps toward the pass, then stopped. I took a couple more and stopped again. My chest felt raw, my throat dry. I stood there, my feet cemented to the ground, just wanting to know the best way to go. Where was Dad's voice now?

"What should I do?"

I waited. No response.

I stared at the ground and tracks stared back up at me. Bear tracks? People tracks? There were no pads or claws, just depressions and no tread marks. But my dad's boots were probably worn slick on the bottoms. They were over twenty years old. Were these his tracks? And if they were, which way was he traveling? I took a few forceful steps and compared my tracks to the ones on the ground. They looked almost the same except mine had tread. Some of them faced the pass and others faced the shore.

The rain came harder. I pulled my hood up, turned away from the pass, and retraced my steps to the outlet of the small lake.

I glanced over my shoulder. A short cut? I didn't know. I didn't know anything except if I hugged the shore that I'd eventually make it to the Sentinels . . . unless I died first. And I hoped my dad would think the same and keep to the shore, too.

As I angled my way down toward Hidden Bay, the open land turned into forest.

On the shore, the breeze barreled into the bay from the southeast. I turned away from the wind and headed toward a small point, hoping to find protection.

My boot-tip caught a root and I fell onto one knee.

I pushed myself up and my knee throbbed like I'd just smashed it on the gym floor.

On the far side of the point, I picked a lone, low-growing branch under a big tree. I dragged deadfall back to the spot and made a slanted roof of sticks and boughs, and then gathered firewood.

I ducked under the roof, kneeling on my good knee, scraped the wet needles away and set down half of my last fire starter stick. The first two matches sparked but wouldn't light. The third one flamed enough to ignite the fire starter stick. I fed it the dud matches and the twigs from my pocket, then bigger sticks until the fire took on a life of its own.

I huddled over the flames and my clothing steamed. My stomach called out for fish. I reached for the fanny pack, then pulled my hand back. "Wood first," I said. "Before it's dark."

So I dragged more deadfall to the shelter, then carried armloads of branches, and pieces of driftwood, my knee throbbing with every step. I put one end of a large log on the coals. Then I dragged another log on from the opposite direction, and settled onto the life vests. But it wasn't a restful rest in this sorry-excuse-of-a-shelter with only a roof and three open sides. The wind ripped through wherever it pleased, tearing at the fire.

Water dripped from one corner of the lean-to. I used a stick and weighted an empty Ziploc baggie under the drip. At least I'd have some drinking water.

Blue and yellow flames curled around the large logs as twilight faded into darkness. The wind died down and the rain settled into a steady pounding on the bay. I draped one of the emergency blankets over my head and shoulders to keep the drips off me. This was gonna be a long night.

CHAPTER 20

LATE the next day, I topped the last headland between Hidden Bay and the open coast. A breeze from the south warned of more wet weather to come.

After a long night of shivering by a small fire, the day so far had been one long trudge. Headland after headland. Climb up. Climb down. At least it wasn't raining right now.

I'd eaten a half fish at mid-day. One fish left in the fanny pack. One fish separating me from starvation.

My blisters must've popped because they stung all the time. And my knee hurt steadily all day. And my neck was itching again. I was pretty much a hazard to my own health. A walking disaster. If I were a horse I'd be first in line at the glue factory.

I sat down. A rocky beach, maybe a half-mile stretch, lay below me before the next point. Once I was on that beach, I'd be outta Hidden Bay. I'd crawl if I had to.

Small goals. That's how I'd make it to the Sentinels.

Today. Out of Hidden Bay.

Tomorrow? I couldn't even imagine tomorrow.

I side-stepped my way down the slope to ease the pressure on my toes. I hoped I'd find a flat spot at the far end of the beach to make camp.

Small waves lapped at my boots as I walked along the shore. I didn't see any tracks but the tide scrubbed the beaches clean every six hours or so. A peach strip of sky at the horizon separated gray rainclouds from the water. If only those clouds would stay over the water.

Then I glimpsed something shiny. It was up in an old strand line bordering the forest. I might've missed it if I hadn't stopped to rub my sore knee. There were specks of plastic in the strand line but they were usually either dull in color or they stood out because they were so obnoxiously different from seaweed and driftwood. But this was twinkling, almost winking at me. Begging me to come check it out.

I dropped my gaff and spear, and walked toward the old strand line.

Where the forest met the beach, seaweed and fragments of driftwood formed a thick, bulging mat. Imbedded in that mat was a silver square a little smaller than a CD case.

I squatted and touched the object. It was some kind of metal. I pulled the knotted seaweed away, then grabbed the metal with both hands and tugged. A mass of seaweed and bite-sized pieces of driftwood tumbled forward and this rotten salty odor invaded my nose.

And in my hands, a stainless steel bowl—about a foot across and six inches deep—smattered with dents.

I sucked in a shallow breath and squinted. Besides the dents, it was just like Mom's popcorn bowl.

Countless times I'd come home from school to the smell of popcorn. Mom's favorite afternoon snack. We'd sit on the couch, sharing popcorn, and tell each other about our days. We still had that bowl, but Dad never used it.

My gaff and spear were half in the water, riding the incoming tide. I lifted them off the water and continued along the coast with the bowl. At the end of the beach, I crossed deer tracks leading from the water's edge straight to the forest. The land was too lumpy for camping, so I kept going even though my toes were screaming to stop.

I scrambled over a rocky point and took in the small cove.

The muscles in my neck tightened.

I'd camped here. With Dad. The day before the accident. Spent two days here, mostly in the tent, because of the lousy weather and big waves.

I dropped the bowl and kicked it, and my toes stung even more. Then I smacked it with my spear.

I picked the bowl back up and walked toward the cove.

Swim for shore.

"I did swim for shore," I said. "The question is, what did you do?" I put my hand on the raincoat fanny pack, then touched his life vest. "If this stuff made it to shore, then you must've too. Right?"

I waited, but the voice didn't come. It never came when I wanted it to. When I actually asked a question.

I reached the back of the cove and sighed. I had work to do.

I faced three huge Sitka spruce, and set the bowl down under the biggest one. Rain pelted the tops of the trees, and started working its way through the branches as I roamed the forest for deadfall.

With arms of lead, I leaned three limbs against the Sitka spruce and dug their ends into the ground so they wouldn't slip, then started laying branches and boughs across them.

I pried rocks from the intertidal for a fire ring, and for throwing. Then I collected firewood. And in the trap of my mind I saw my dad bobbing in the waves and wished I'd seen what I needed to see, then maybe we wouldn't have had an accident. And I wished I'd gone on that bike ride with my mom.

———

It was a small shelter, barely five feet tall next to the tree. About six feet long and four feet wide.

I used the dry twigs in my raincoat pocket to light a fire. I fed it larger sticks, then took my bowl to the small stream Dad and I had used.

I squatted, filled the bowl partway, rinsed it, filled it again, then drank a whole bowlful of water. And then drank another just because I could. Because I thought it was so cool that I didn't have to scoop water with my hands twenty times just to quench my thirst.

I refilled the bowl and walked back to camp.

The raincoat with the fish lay next to the fire. The fish I'd hoped would get me to the Sentinels.

It all came down to food.

No food meant no life.

At home, when I opened the freezer to get some ice cream, or made myself a peanut butter sandwich, or some scrambled eggs, it never crossed my mind that I was eating to survive. I was just having a snack, or breakfast or whatever.

And who cared if I didn't finish the sandwich and tossed some of it out, or if I left eggs on my plate. There was always more. Now I wished I

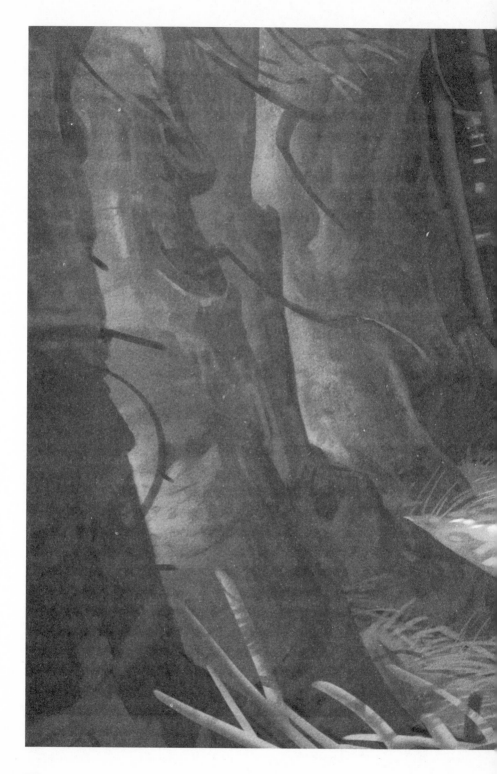

had all the remains of all the sandwiches I'd never finished. I'd even take the cabbage, beans, and broccoli—the ever-present leftovers on my plate when Mom was still alive. We had a big garden with a seven-foot-tall fence to keep the moose out, but Dad hadn't touched it since Mom died. It was all overgrown with fireweed and saplings. But if I wanted to change that, I could. I didn't have to wait for Dad to decide to fix up the garden. Just like I didn't have to wait for him to learn how to play guitar. To play my mom's guitar. When I get home, I just need to do those things. Just like right now. If I wanted a shelter, I had to build one.

I took a hunk of fish and put it into the bowl, raked some coals to the side of the main fire, and centered the bowl on top of them.

"Fish soup," I said. "I'll eat hot fish soup."

The water got a brownish tinge to it as more of the fish gave itself over to the boiling liquid, and a rich, fishy odor filled my sorry little shelter.

I put on my ragged wool gloves, lifted the bowl off the coals and set it on the ground.

Little bits of salmon hung suspended in the liquid, like the silt in the Tanana River in Fairbanks. We'd scooped river water for a science experiment last year. At first it seemed like there was more silt than water, but after it settled to the bottom of the container, I was surprised by how little there was.

After a few minutes I took my gloves off and felt the side of the bowl. It was warm but not hot, so I lifted it. I let the steam warm my face, then gulped a couple mouthfuls of broth and set the bowl down.

I wanted it to last forever. To sit here and sip warm broth until a boat buzzed into this cove and found me. A boat with my dad on it.

After the broth was gone, I ate the clumps of warm, mushy fish, then licked my fingers.

Week-old, mushed-up, boiled-up salmon—I loved it, every mouthful. I'd eat it three times a day if I could. Or twice a day, I'd settle for that. Even once a day would be great, as long as I knew it was coming.

The rain didn't let up. A continuous drip of water formed at one corner of the shelter, so I put the bowl under the drip.

I draped an emergency blanket over my shoulders and leaned toward the fire, keeping the blanket open a little so it'd trap the hot air.

The bowl, I thought. It rocks. And it couldn't have come from very far away, because once it filled with water it would've sunk. Probably fell out of a boat, but when? Or someone left it on the beach. How long ago?

Maybe it really was a gift from Mom. I felt my cheeks lift a little. But how could it be? Like it really couldn't be the bowl we used at home. Like one of those *Hunger Games* magic parachutes had delivered it. But still, here it was, and I'd found it mostly buried in dead seaweed.

The warm air was building under the blanket, surrounding me while the broth warmed me from the inside. Sleep. I just wanted to sleep. Could fall asleep right now.

Sleep and dream about being with Mom.

Eating popcorn.

With butter.

And salt.

Maybe even hear Mom's voice.

I heard a pop, and a crackling noise. And I smelled the popcorn. I was there, warm, with her.

I felt the heat on my face and jerked my head back.

My blanket. A whole quarter of it was gone. Burned up on the coals.

Another stupid mistake.

I'm just lucky the whole thing hadn't gone up in flames or melted onto me. Or that I hadn't collapsed onto the fire.

One of my mom's friends passed out by a campfire and burned up her hands. She was standing up and fainted. Fell right into the fire. She had to wear bandages for weeks, and have surgery. "If I burned myself like that," I whispered, "I'd be done."

I had Dad to thank for the blankets. For everything. Not just the knives and matches and fishing lures, but what he'd taught me. And not just skills, but ideas about how to live. And Mom, too. Her songs were all about living, and risk taking, and paying attention.

Yeah, I'd made some mistakes, but I was still alive.

The less I have, I realized, the more thankful I am for what I do have.

Like the bowl. Who'd ever think to be thankful that they had a bowl?

And out here, I wasn't using my bowl as just a bowl—I used it as a pot, too.

The bowl was half-filled from the drip. I raked some coals to the side of the fire, flattened them a little and put the bowl on. I slipped another hunk of fish in the water.

Only a half a fish left.

Never enough food.

And firewood. The pile wasn't as big as I'd like it to be. I stayed warm enough when I hovered over the fire with my blanket open, but I couldn't trust myself to not fall asleep and land in the flames.

If only I could take a break from this. Just for one day. If I could be back at home for one day. Just to sleep in my bed. And rest, and eat, and take a long, hot shower. And put band-aids on my blisters and some stuff on my neck to keep it from itching. Just one day to block it all out and pretend everything was normal.

━━━

The next morning I stirred the coals in my fire ring and a few red embers surfaced. I must've fallen into a deep sleep. Deep enough that I wasn't constantly stoking the fire. And I hadn't seen Dad bobbing in the waves. I hadn't seen Mom either.

I placed twigs I had dried by the fire onto the coals, and blew until tiny flames licked upward.

I fed the flames with larger and larger sticks.

Warmth.

Warmth.

Warmth.

When you slept were you somehow shielded from the cold? I mean, I had crashed but now that I was awake, I was cold. So many things I didn't understand.

I stuck my feet in front of the fire. They had way more blisters than normal skin.

The bowl had filled with rainwater overnight, so I put it on the fire. When the water had warmed just a little I scooped handfuls onto my feet. It felt like I was throwing boiling oil on them, but I thought it was a good idea to rinse them. They were really red. Like maybe they were infected. I dabbed some warm water on my neck too. The swan bite had closed up but the skin around it itched. I knew the less I touched it the less it would itch but it was hard not to scratch it. Especially at night when I was sleepy. It was just natural to scratch an itch.

I had to be my own doctor out here. My own everything. And since I was my own everything that meant I was the boss. I could do whatever I wanted: cuss, scream, run naked, scratch an itch until it bled, whatever.

But all I wanted was to stay here, and fill my stomach with hot liquid. Just for a day. To rest. To let my blisters air out by the fire.

I'd need more wood if I stayed. But I'd only have to wear my boots while I collected it. Then I could really let my feet heal. And if I could keep my hands off my neck, maybe the itching sensation would go away too.

If I could start off the next day feeling fresh, then the Sentinels wouldn't feel so far away.

When I was tired from walking and my blisters were burning, the negative thoughts crept in. The thoughts that said I'd never make it to the Sentinels. It was just too far.

I pulled my socks and boots on, then set off to search for more wood. Every step hurt. I hauled a few loads of firewood to camp, and worked up a sweat, but I was warm as long as I kept moving. And yeah, the sweat made my neck itch even more, but so far, I hadn't scratched it yet today.

The rain faded to a fine mist, and hints of blue appeared in the sky. Just a little more wood, and then it'd be boots-off, feet-by-the-fire time. Maybe I'd even take a bath with warm water. And then tomorrow I'd be rested and I'd get an early start for the Sentinels.

On a trip upslope in search of more wood, I got dizzy, a little light-headed, so I just stopped and took deep breaths. Stopping seemed to work because I could always keep going afterwards, even if it was only for a few more steps before I had to stop again.

It was when I was standing still, taking deep breaths, partway up a forested hillside, that I heard the scratching noise.

BEFORE THE ACCIDENT

I kept pulling for the next point, rain peppering my face, salty spray burning my eyes. I squeezed my eyes tight and wiped my sleeve across them, hoping to ease the burning sensation. I only had them closed for a couple seconds, but when I opened them a monster of a rock reef lay right in front of us. White water drained through and around the razor-sharp formations.

I pointed with my paddle and yelled, "Dad, straight ahead, a big rock! Turn! Turn!"

CHAPTER 21

I WORKED my way upslope toward the downed tree where I thought the noise was coming from. It was a monster of a tree, the top of the trunk even with my shoulders, and it'd taken a bunch of smaller trees down with it, creating a jungle of deadfall.

I stopped to rest, and heard the scratching noise again. Up by the root wad, I thought, that's where it's coming from.

"Hey bear. Hey bear," I called.

I heard it again. And shouted "hey bear" again, but saw nothing. If it was a bear, I think it would've run away or come to check me out. But you never know. Sometimes Dad would get quiet when he'd hear a noise and sometimes he'd make noise back. I'm not even sure how he decided.

Whatever it was either didn't know I was here, or didn't care, because the scratching stopped and started regardless of whether I yelled. So I decided to just shut up.

Maybe it was a squirrel or a porcupine. I didn't know.

I moved parallel to the huge tree and climbed over branches and smaller trees that lay on the ground, pinned by the fallen giant.

I stopped just downslope from the root wad. Even that was huge. Probably twelve feet high.

I heard a fury of scratching, and then quiet. Then more scratching.

I moved closer. The scratching stopped.

I reached the edge of the root wad and stopped again to listen.

Nothing.

It must know I'm here, I thought. Whatever it is. It doesn't want me here. Doesn't want me to know it's here. I'm not sure I want to be here. But I had to know. Wanted to know. Just like figuring out that the fish ran with the tide, and that storms came from the south, every little thing I learned was helping me. Plus, I was just plain curious.

In the center of the root wad, a massive, square-shaped boulder, crisscrossed with roots, hovered over the hole that used to be its home.

I stepped to the side of the root wad, peered into the hole, then jumped back. My heel caught on a rock and I landed on my butt.

I stood up and took a couple steps forward.

Lying on its stomach, eyes wide open, was a small Sitka black-tail deer.

I leaned forward to get a closer look and the deer's hind legs exploded, kicking at the dirt wall, causing chunks to break off and roll into the hole.

The deer kicked again and again but never stood on its front legs.

It must've hurt itself.

Broken its front legs.

Could've fallen in the hole and hurt its legs.

Food. Meat. All that meat.

Kill it. Kill it. Kill it, my mind screamed.

The deer kicked, like it could read my mind, and then grew still again.

"But you're so small," I said. "A fawn."

And no antlers. Probably female. A baby girl, born this year.

She had a white patch of fur on her throat. And a black nose and tail. And mixed black and brown fur between her eyes. And cottony-white fur inside her ears. Walnut brown eyes.

She's beautiful.

Kill her.

She's beautiful and I needed to kill her.

I shook my head.

But I *needed* to do it.

I hadn't thought about beauty when I'd stalked the porcupine in the dark and stabbed it. I'd just done it. But to kill an animal that you could look in the eye? And a deer? It felt more like a person than the porcupine. Just like the porcupine felt more like a person than the salmon.

But the deer, there it was, all that meat. A goldmine of meat.

And the deer couldn't survive in the hole. Even if it got out, with two injured legs...I shook my head again.

If I didn't kill it, something else would, like a bear. And a bear might eat it alive. Eat while it screamed in agony, the deer feeling every bite.

I searched the area for something substantial, then pried a rock the size of a salmon from the ground.

I watched the deer kick the dirt wall, and waited until it became still.

My heart hammered away. I raised the rock over my head with both hands.

Right on top of the head. One hard hit. Just one, and it'd be over. No suffering.

I couldn't miss.

I slammed the rock downward and let go.

But the deer jerked sideways, and the rock grazed the side of its head. And then it kicked harder than it had before. It rose up on its front legs for a second, then collapsed again.

I could see a dark area where the rock had hit.

Blood.

Must be blood.

My spear.

I ran downslope, light-headed, on rubbery legs and burning feet.

The sun was peeking through the clouds.

I was energized. Like I'd just been given another chance at life.

But I worried about a bear finding the deer. I needed to get back there— fast.

At my shelter, I threw two pieces of wood onto the bed of coals, grabbed my spear, and started upslope.

Out of breath, at the edge of the hole, I faced the deer. My body trembled.

I had to stab it. But where? I knew hunters shot moose in the heart and lungs. But I couldn't get a shot like that because of the way the deer was sitting.

The neck. I'd go for the neck; it'd worked with the porcupine. And it'd died quickly.

I jabbed the spear toward the deer, and grazed its neck. The deer kicked harder and moved from side to side and rose up on its front legs for a second, then fell again. It turned its head so it was looking me right in the eye. Staring through me. My dad's face flashed before my eyes. I blinked and then I was staring at the deer again.

You can respect a life and still take it.

I needed to wait until the deer was still and then thrust hard—from close range. As hard as I could.

I had to kill if I wanted to live.

I imagined stabbing the deer so hard that the spear poked in one side of its neck, then out the other. I closed my eyes, saw myself doing it, then opened them.

It's kill, or eventually be killed. As much as I didn't want to do it, I knew I had to.

The deer looked all cute and cuddly, but it wasn't. Given a chance, that deer would kick me until I couldn't stand. Animals didn't just lie down and die. Especially trapped, injured animals. Just like that porcupine, or all the fish I'd killed. They fought for every last gasp of air, and in any way they could.

When the deer stopped kicking, I knelt at the edge of the hole. The deer kicked again, then lay still. I clutched the spear in both hands about a foot from the base. I raised it over my head, and to the side.

I took a breath, held it, then thrust the spear downward as hard as I could and felt it grinding into the deer's neck.

The deer rose up and jerked its head to one side. The spear was yanked from my hands and thrust back at me.

CHAPTER 22

I HUGGED my chest. I was cold.

I felt around for the blankets, but couldn't find them. Then I opened my eyes and this pale light made me squint.

The moon. The full moon.

I tried to sit up, but one of my legs was dangling in space from the knee down. So I scooted backwards and tried again.

I succeeded, but sitting up sent my head into pound-mode. Like someone had shoved a balloon inside my ear and was inflating it.

The deer, I remembered.

The deer.

The deer.

The deer.

And, the spear.

But my head—that balloon was gonna pop.

I ran my hand along the left side of my head and felt a lump. I probed it gently with my fingers, searched for moisture, for blood, and found none.

I let my arm fall to my side and it bumped into the end of the spear. I gave it a pull, but met resistance.

I'd lost control of the spear, I remembered that much. I touched the side of my head, and nodded. Clocked by my own weapon.

I followed the spear, and could just make out the form of the deer in the hole. It wasn't moving. It had to be dead.

Had it lived long after I'd stabbed it? Had it suffered? Then I remembered that it was already suffering. It was gonna die anyway. But I knew that I'd try to kill a healthy deer, too.

I'd kill any animal—a baby seal, a bald eagle, ducklings, a sea otter pup. I didn't care where the food came from as long as it kept on coming.

I crawled out of the circle of dirt surrounding the hole, then stood. The large tree that had fallen created an opening in the tree tops where the moonlight flowed freely. Beyond, the forest was inky black, cut up by slices of moonlight. I looked in the direction of my camp. I thought I could find it. I hugged myself again, then pulled my hat out of my raincoat pocket and put it on.

But I couldn't just leave the deer because a bear might get it. I needed a fire. Right here. Right now.

I followed the fallen tree to a pile of sticks and branches that I'd collected and then dropped when I first approached the root wad hours ago.

The damp branches would catch in an already burning fire, or on a bed of hot coals, but I needed dry wood.

Pick a piece that you know is dead and start shaving. Make the shavings as thin as you can. It'll take some effort, but sometimes it's the only way.

How did my mind do that? I didn't control it, but what did? If it really was just all in my head, then I guess my mind was smarter than me.

Too bad he hadn't yelled, *"Watch out!"* when that spear was coming toward me.

I grabbed a branch, took the knife from my pocket, and started whittling. Every time the knife skipped on the wood, my head pounded.

When I had a pile of shavings the size of a softball, I held the lighter under them.

The shavings curled, then caught fire. I slipped twigs and small sticks between the flames, and nursed my fire out of the danger zone into a small blaze. I added larger branches, which steamed at first, but eventually caught fire.

I wanted my life vests and blankets, the last of my fish, and my bowl, so I picked my way downslope in the direction of my camp, hoping to use the firelight as a guide for my return trip.

▬

In the morning, I sat next to the deer-hole in the full sun. I knew I needed to keep the meat as cool as possible, which meant I had work to do. Work that I'd never done before.

A dark area lay around the deer's head and neck where she had bled to death. An image of my mom, her smile framed by her bike helmet flashed into my brain. Did she bleed like this? I took a breath and pushed it out. I needed to concentrate on what I was doing.

I took the spear in both hands and pulled. The carcass moved with it, so I squatted next to the hole and hauled up on the spear. If I could just get it out of the hole, that was the first step.

So I kept hauling, and saw one of its ears peeking over the edge. I pulled harder, bent away from the deer with all my weight. Now its head was over the lip of the hole. I kept pulling and leaning but then tumbled backwards with the spear. I hit the ground, and the butt of the spear smashed into my chin.

I threw the spear down and grabbed my chin, held it with my hand for a moment, then released it.

My hand came back moist and red.

With my thumb I felt a curved gash just under one side of my jawbone. I couldn't tell how deep it was, but my thumb came back coated with blood. Dark red blood.

I pressed my palm into the wound. I just wanted it to stop bleeding. I didn't know how deep it was, but the blood was flowing like it was coming from an open faucet. I could feel it on my palm.

Some razor-sharp rocks had sliced my mom deep. Did she try to stop the bleeding or had she passed out immediately? I knew you could only lose so much blood, but didn't know how much. My mom had bled through her stomach and her thighs. An image of her covered in blood took over my mind. I felt my stomach clench, then my mouth was open and I was gagging but nothing was coming up.

I wiped the sweat from my forehead, then pressed my palm back into the wound. Why hadn't I seen the danger in what I'd been doing? Another stupid mistake. I took one breath. Then another. I still needed to get that deer out of the hole, gut it and skin it, but if I bled to death while doing it, that'd be pointless. And just sitting here my chin was leaking pretty bad, about a hundred times worse than my swan bite had.

Your blood is your life. You lose enough of it and you no longer exist.

..s how my mom died. That's how the deer died. That's how I might die. *Use what you've got. Use what you know. That's all you can do.*

I felt moisture on the palm of my hand so I increased the pressure. My heart pounded like I'd just sprinted up a mountain. I took a breath. "Slow it down. Slow it down." The faster my heart beat the more blood I'd lose. Constant pressure. Relentless pressure. But I needed my hands free.

I unzipped my raincoat and took it off. Then I pulled my pile jacket off. The back of my hand grazed the wound, and it came back bloody.

I pulled my long underwear shirt off, which was like having a skunk crawl over my face. That shirt was my second skin. I never took it off.

It was stiff with layers of dried sweat, so I bunched it up in my hands to loosen it, then spread it on top of my raincoat, and as I rolled it up, leaving the sleeves free, a drop of blood hit the back of my hand, then another, and another.

Using the sleeves, I tied the skunk-shirt-bandage over the top of my head and under my chin, with the rolled up part pressing into the wound.

I saw the red draining from my mom's legs and stomach. Saw it soaking the ground. If only someone had been there to put pressure on her wounds to keep the life from draining out of her. If only the driver would have stopped. If only I'd gone on that bike ride.

I reached for my pile jacket, then stopped. Even with the sun, the cool air prickled my skin. Goosebumps covered my arms. But gutting a deer could get messy.

I cinched down the sleeves of the skunk-bandage and adjusted the knot so it centered on the top of my head and hoped it would do the job.

Okay, if the deer's too heavy to haul out of there, I thought, then I'll just gut it in the hole, then haul it out. It'd be lighter.

I eased my legs over the edge of the hole, and dropped to the bottom.

My hand brushed against the fur. Soft like a cat's fur. I knew it wasn't going to spring back to life, but it was spooky being next to an animal that looked like it was just asleep. Like I could shake it and it'd wake up.

I closed my eyes. "Just like a fish, or a porcupine," I whispered. "Just slit the belly, clean the sucker out, and get it back to camp."

I pushed the deer against the side of the hole to increase my leverage. The ends of the sleeves on my skunk-bandage kept grazing my eyes, so I tucked them under themselves.

I took a breath and poked the knife into the white furry belly and slit it up to its sternum. Some of the intestines poured out, partially covering my rubber boots.

I tilted my head away from the mess on my boots, took another breath and told myself, "don't stop now."

I reached inside the deer, and pulled and scooped and scraped, trying to get all the organs out. Then, I cut along the inside of the ribs and worked the lungs and heart out.

I turned away and heaved, but my stomach was empty. I guess the air was pretty rank down here between the guts and the skunk bandage. I stood up and sucked in the freshest air I could.

I hoped I'd gotten everything out of the deer to keep the meat in good condition. I'd heard stories from Mr. Haskins about meat spoiling when someone like me, who didn't know jack about what they were doing, cut into an animal.

Keep the guts from spilling on the meat, that's what I remembered. And get the skin off the animal. That would help cool the meat. My dad wasn't a hunter. He loved fishing and talked about taking up hunting someday, but never had. Billy's dad had a riverboat and took him hunting last year. Billy didn't say much about the trip. Just that his dad was a jerk with a drinking problem even when they were away from home.

I tried lifting the deer out of the hole, but it kept falling on top of me, and the guts. I cringed every time the deer hit the guts.

This was my meat. No way could I ruin it. Without the deer, I may as well turn the knife on myself.

I tried lying on my stomach at the lip of the hole and pulling the deer out, but could barely reach it, and couldn't get enough leverage.

I stood up and looked around. I needed to get the deer away from the gut pile, which I knew would attract bears.

I leaned the spear on the edge of the hole, took a couple of pieces of rope out of my survival kit, and climbed back down, my boots squishing through the intestines. I tied the front legs of the deer together and slipped the spear through the rope. I lifted one end of the spear, rested it on the lip of the hole, then did the same with the other end so the deer just hung there.

I hoisted myself out again. I tried brushing the dirt off my bare chest and arms but just smeared it around. I mean, it was a combination of deer guts and blood, my sweat, and dirt. I was bear bait.

I touched my skunk-bandage and felt moisture right under the wound—it'd soaked through at least four or five layers of sweaty cloth. An image of my mom's white biking shirt saturated with blood invaded my mind, and I wondered what was flashing through her mind if and when she realized she wasn't going to make it. What do you do with the last moment of your life when you are alone?

I grabbed the spear—a hand on each side of the hooves—and started pulling. The deer's front hooves came over the lip of the hole. Its head appeared. Then the deer lay in the dirt next to the hole.

"Yes," I said. "Yes. Yes. Yes. All right. I'm gonna be all right."

I draped the small deer over my bare shoulders and started downslope, dodging deadfall. I figured it weighed about sixty pounds, as much as a sled dog.

Just outside my shelter, I dropped the deer, then jogged back upslope for the rest of my stuff.

I was gonna put the pile jacket on but still didn't feel cold as long as I was moving, so I just kept moving. Plus, I was a stinking wreck and didn't want any of my clothes touching me right now.

I collected wood for strengthening and enlarging my shelter, and for burning. Then I broke boughs and dragged them to my shelter.

I leaned more big sticks against the giant Sitka spruce, and laid branches and boughs across them, until my shelter wrapped halfway around the tree.

I stacked boughs in the back entrance to close up the space. I thought about putting a fire ring there, but the shelter bent around so much I didn't think it'd be worth it. But I couldn't just leave it open for the bears.

I lit a fire just after the sun dipped below the ridge behind camp.

I knew I was supposed to eat and sleep in different places. But I couldn't let the deer out of my sight for long stretches of time. A bear might get it. I'd use it for a pillow if I had to.

I had to skin this thing, so I made a cut below the neck and across the back, then pulled on the skin. It started to peel back, but then the meat started coming off with it, so I held the skin with one hand, and using my knife, cut away at the flesh.

I kept working, pulling on the skin, using the knife to separate it from the meat until I'd exposed most of the flesh. There was still some skin on the lower legs. And the head, I didn't know what to do with it so I just left it on. But the body and upper legs were clean.

I added another round of sticks to the fire, then brought in boughs and covered the floor of the shelter.

I hadn't eaten any of the deer, but just knowing I had it had somehow energized me. And that made me think about how powerful thoughts could be. I didn't quite understand why I was able to push myself when I had two head injuries, blistered feet, and had been starving since leaving Fish Camp. But I thought if I could figure it out a little more—that it would be useful. I mean, what if I didn't know where my next meal was coming from? Why couldn't I have as much energy then as I did now? I'd only gotten dizzy once since I killed the deer, but yesterday I was stopping every ten steps to rest.

I carried the skinned deer into the shelter, and set it against the big spruce at the very back. The meat was cool to the touch. And that made me relax a little bit, like maybe it wasn't rotting from sitting in the hole all night.

I built up the fire, then stripped until the only thing I was wearing was the skunk bandage. It was still moist under the wound, but at least it hadn't dripped.

My blister-covered feet picked up spruce needles as I picked my way toward the small stream. This was gonna be my first official bath since the accident. I wished I didn't have the gash under my chin. I really wanted to dunk my head and scrub my hair but didn't want to mess with the bandage.

At the bank, I eased my way in until I was standing shin deep, then bent and started splashing water between my legs and onto my chest and just kept splashing and scrubbing until my skin prickled with the cold.

The meat bobbed in the slow boil. I held my nose over the bowl, and just kept inhaling. I had my pile jacket on. No boots, no socks, and the skunk bandage was still tied around my head. I'd scrubbed my long johns at the stream and now they were propped on a branch beside the fire, steaming.

Besides my head, I actually felt clean.

I pinned the meat with one knife and cut it into hunks with the other, then speared them into my mouth. One piece after another, like I was part of an assembly line.

Stab meat.

Insert in mouth.

Chew with mouth only open a little so bandage stays in place.

Swallow.

Repeat until bowl has only broth, then refill.

I turned to the deer, just a dark blob at the edge of the firelight. I smiled. All this from just one kill. And I thought about how lucky I was that I'd heard the noise. And then I thought about the bowl, and how lucky I was that I'd spotted it.

And then thought, no, it's only part luck.

And part learning how to look and listen.

I'd spotted that silver square because it was out of place. I knew what a strand line was supposed to look like, with the dull greens and browns, and pale yellows.

And with the deer? I hadn't just found it. I'd taken action.

But getting knocked out, and then waking up hours later with a dead deer in the hole without a bear on top of it? Well, maybe that was a bit of luck. And the gash under my chin? Yeah, it was sore, and I didn't know how deep it was, but I hadn't bled to death, yet.

Maybe my blisters were partly responsible. If my feet weren't so torn up, I wouldn't have decided to stay here an extra day. Then I started thinking about why my feet were torn up, and I realized that all this stuff was connected in more ways than one.

It wasn't some straight connect-the-dots-line where only one thing causes another.

I cut another couple inches off the flank and plopped it into the broth.

Later, with a belly full of broth and meat, I snatched bits of sleep between keeping the fire stoked, understanding that this deer was my life.

THE ACCIDENT

"Here we go," my dad yelled.

I felt the kayak jerk sideways. Now we were parallel to the waves on the outside of the rock reef. I reached forward to paddle, but this huge mother of a wave broke broadside on the kayak and buried my arm in the surf. The wall of water popped my spray skirt free from the combing and poured into my cockpit.

I tried to sit up straight, but the boat was leaning toward the waves.

"Paddle!" Dad yelled.

I lifted my paddle and dug into the surf. Then the second wave hit, and I heard a crack. I leaned away from the rock and suddenly I was in the water upside down.

CHAPTER 23

Since the accident, the sun was something I'd glimpsed between rainstorms, but now, for the fourth day in a row, it filtered through the forest in long golden rays like it'd always been here. Steam drifted from moss-covered logs. Out on the beach, the dark rocks were warm to the touch, but you could still freeze to death at night if you didn't have a fire.

I'd washed and dried all my clothes except for my shirt, which was still wrapped under my chin.

The sun was warm, but the north wind kept things cool enough, so the deer hadn't rotted yet. At least I didn't have to worry about flies laying eggs on the meat like I would've in the summer. Or yellow jackets swarming.

I stuffed myself with hunks of boiled deer meat and drank the broth, figuring this was the best way to get all I could from the deer. I had to keep tightening the skunk bandage around my head because it loosened up every time I moved my jaw to chew, and I was eating all the time.

I cut thin strips of deer meat and dried them on an alder grill until they were almost crispy. I had thirty strips, each about three inches long by one inch wide. These I stored in my shelter in one of my Ziploc bags, keeping it open to allow the air to circulate.

My new plan: dry as much deer meat as I could and then make a push for the Sentinels.

I snatched bits of sleep between keeping the fire stoked. I'd dry the deer meat during the day, then build the fire up big at night. I hadn't seen any bears at this camp, not even fresh scat in the forest, but figured that fire was the main thing that would keep them away from the deer if any wandered through.

I counted backwards and guessed it'd been at least a week since I'd left Fish Camp, and according to the marks on my spear, thirty-two days since the accident.

I was still as skinny as a starving chicken, but I had some energy. And I used it to collect wood and boughs, and to cut and dry deer meat. My feet were healing too, with a thin layer of new skin covering some of my blisters. And my swan bite had finally stopped itching.

My shelter was starting to sag in the middle from the weight of the boughs. I thought about trying to fix it, but right now I needed to deal with the skunk bandage. Sometimes my wound throbbed like it had its own heart. I wanted to know what was going on under there, but was scared to remove the bandage only to have blood start gushing. The shirt was crusty with dried blood on the outside, but I hadn't stuck my fingers underneath to see what was going on 'cause I didn't want to open the wound up if it was healing.

I saw the clouds building to the south, and knew this might be my only chance to wash my shirt and actually be able to dry it. Plus, I wanted to wear my shirt the way it was supposed to be worn. I missed that layer right next to my skin, something the air couldn't get under. And I was still a little freaked about wearing a bloody bandage 'cause I thought bears might be attracted by the smell.

Wash that thing. Bears like blood. Period.

I untied the sleeves from the top of my head, and peeled the skunk bandage off my face and the underside of my jaw, but when I got to the wound the shirt stuck, like it was part of my skin.

I held the bunched-up shirt under my jaw as I walked to the stream. If the gash was actually closing, I wanted to do all I could to keep it from opening up.

I lay on my belly and dipped my chin into the water.

I tugged gently on the shirt, but it still wouldn't let go. I sunk my head in the cold water farther, and shook it back and forth, and kept gently pulling on the shirt, and little by little it came free. I set the shirt on the shore and stuck my head under and raked my fingers across my scalp. The cold water plugged my ears, made it feel like my head was gonna explode.

It needed a scrubbing, but having my head under freaked me out a little, so I bobbed it up and down and took a gulp of air each time and just kept raking.

I sat up and shook my hair, kind of like a dog does when it gets out of the water. Then I patted the wound with my fingers and they came back pink.

I took a breath. Not what I wanted to see. But pink was better than red.

I wished I could see what was going on, and then I thought, the bowl. I jogged back to my shelter, grabbed the empty bowl and peeked into it, but saw only a blurry image among the dents.

I flipped the bowl over and caught an image of my face on the side of the bowl. The image was small, about as long as my index finger, but pretty clear. I could make out a reddish smudge where the wound was. And within that smudge, a curved red line. I ran my hand along my neck below the wound. It came back clean. I touched the wound and my fingertips turned pink again. At least it wasn't gushing. A little pink, I could live with. Like I had a choice. Then I tilted the bowl to have a look at my swan bite. All I saw was a narrow straight line below my ear lobe.

Back at the creek, I scrubbed the shirt, watched the water turn pink, and wrung it out. And I kept rinsing and wringing the shirt until the water looked almost clear.

It was hard to keep my fingers off the gash, even though I knew that the more I touched it the more likely I'd mess it up or get it dirty. I was about to head back to my shelter when I heard a splash downstream. I stood still, looking with eyes, listening with my ears, and trying to just feel whatever it was that was out there.

I took a breath.

Be like a tree—still.

I heard another splash, then a hump of brown fur appeared in the middle of the creek.

CHAPTER 24

A LONGISH head popped out of the water about thirty feet from me, and let out a call that sounded like a muffled giggle. Then another head popped up, and another. Until there were seven in all. And they were all making these giggle-sounds, like they were having a conversation. One of them crawled up the bank on the opposite side of the creek from where I was standing and produced the loudest giggle yet. It had some gray fur mixed in with the brown. It pulled itself along on its belly for a couple of lunges and then turned and spoke again.

River otters, I thought. A family of river otters. I'd seen solitary river otters a few times around Fairbanks, but never a whole family of them. Unlike sea otters, which are more rounded and live off shellfish, river otters are slender and eat mostly fish, but they'll make a meal of ducks too, if they can catch them. The otters in the creek were chattering back and forth, their heads turning toward each other and the gray one on shore was getting louder and louder.

Come on, I thought. Follow the old guy. He probably knows what he's doing. And like I could control them with my mind, they started one by one up the bank taking the exact route the gray one had taken. They were still talking their giggle-talk and were now bunched up on a small mound almost directly across from me. I had remained completely still so either they didn't know I was here, or didn't care. The gray one started moving again, traveling away from the creek.

No, I thought, don't go. Don't leave me. And I let out a couple of giggles, trying my best to imitate them. They all turned as one and seemed to focus in on me. First one, then another and another giggled back, until they were all giggling. I let out another giggle and that set them to giggling louder and louder.

I wasn't sure what we were talking about. I just wanted to keep the conversation going. They were stretching their long necks like they were trying to see me better. Then I realized that I hadn't moved a muscle besides the ones controlling my vocal cords so maybe they actually hadn't seen me yet. Maybe they were trying to figure out where the sound was coming from. If you heard someone say hello but didn't see them, then heard the "hello" again and still didn't see anyone, wouldn't you be curious? I would.

I took a tentative step toward them and the giggling ceased like it'd been cut by a knife. Then it was replaced by something like screams.

"Wait," I said. "Wait." I did the giggle-noise again but their screams just grew louder, and all together the family of river otters disappeared into the forest and my heart sank. I mean, besides my dad's voice, I was actually talking to some people. Well, not people exactly, but still, I was hanging out with them.

If only I hadn't moved. But I couldn't have stood there forever. Still, they'd talked back to me in giggle-talk before they'd seen me. They'd accepted me, that's how it felt. And maybe they would come back and maybe they wouldn't panic and scream and run when they realized that I didn't want to hurt them, that I just wanted to be with them.

And then I thought of the deer I'd killed. Could they sense I was a killer? Is that why they ran? But they were meat eaters too. I'd watched a video of a river otter eating a salmon. It started from the fish's head and ripped and tore and swallowed.

The next day the clouds started dumping rain. But it was a colder rain, like it might change to snow. And the air had that metal taste you get before it snows.

All the fingers in my gloves had holes. My rain pants had split between the legs. And the heels in my socks were see-through thin.

In Fairbanks sometimes we'd skip fall, or have it for a week or two, and go right to winter. Once you got into September you just never knew when, as my dad likes to say, "the hammer would come down."

Out here, I didn't know what to expect, but I didn't have any winter boots or gloves. I didn't have any winter anything. If the hammer of winter dropped, I'd be pounded over and over.

I spent most of the day inside, drying deer meat. And thinking.

Since the accident I'd turned into a nomad. Traveling until I found food and then staying until the food source disappeared. I knew I needed to get to the Sentinels, knew that it was unlikely I'd see anyone anyplace else, but my day-to-day actions were driven by basic survival.

And really, they were almost the same thing.

I had to concentrate day to day—sometimes moment to moment—on survival to have any chance of reaching the Sentinels. So, the colder weather worried me, but I knew I had to get the most I could from the deer. It didn't matter if there were ten miles between me and the Sentinels or fifty. I still had to feed myself, build up my strength and stay warm. And take as much deer jerky as I could carry when I left because there was no guarantee I'd have anything else to eat. I still had my dad's Meal Pack bars, but those weren't for me.

The farther from the day of the kill, the longer I boiled the meat before eating, and the longer I let the strips smoke and dry on the alder, hoping to kill any germs. I didn't want to puke my guts out from eating rotten meat.

I cut some deer skin into thin strips and soaked them in warm water until they were flexible, then inserted them into the fingers of my gloves. When the strips dried they stiffened up again, but were held in place and shaped by the fingers of the gloves. That was cool. But I didn't know what to do with the rest of the skin, so I left it alone and dried more deer meat.

And I thought and thought about the big trees at the southern end of the island—the Sentinels—a place my parents had gone together. I could kinda see why my parents thought it was special. Maybe if my parents hadn't planned on taking me there, my dad wouldn't have felt like he had to do it. But it did make him start acting like a normal person again, like he actually cared about me. And then he disappeared after he'd come back to life.

"Disappeared," I said. "He didn't disappear." I tried to wipe the thought from my mind. "We just haven't found each other yet."

If I could just get there and stay under those big trees. If a boat was gonna come across, that's where it'd come because it was the shortest distance from the mainland. And dad—that's where he'd go. But something else drew me there, too. Like I was gonna learn something, or understand something, but didn't know what it was about.

When I pictured myself on this island surrounded by ocean, and then all that empty country on the mainland, I felt so small. When I was little, my mom used to read me that *Horton Hears a Who* book by Dr. Suess. And she'd tell me that there were so many tiny things, whole worlds underneath rocks, or in puddles. And then later she told me the Earth was like a speck of dust in the universe, and I didn't quite get what she meant until Mr. Haskins did this thing where he showed us the Earth in relation to the universe. Then I thought it was cool. But I understood it even better now. If the Earth was a speck of dust in the universe, then I was less than a speck of dust on the Earth. And that made me think of God. I mean, if there was a God that created the universe, then who created God? And if there was another God that created the God that created the universe, then who created that God? That whole thing ran through my mind again. But if there wasn't a God, then how could I find my mom's popcorn bowl way out here? And what about the deer in the hole, and Dad's voice? Still, those things didn't prove anything.

Maybe God wasn't some guy that controlled things. Maybe God was some kind of power or presence. Or maybe it was just within people. Yeah, I still didn't know if God existed or not. But who did? How could anyone actually know that?

One thing I did know was this. My dad had done a brave thing by coming out here and facing the memories.

He was moving on. Healing. We both were. This was the start. I needed to finish the trip or at least try as hard as I could, and if the trip finished me, well, at least I'd tried, really tried. I owed that to my dad. As much as I wanted to, I couldn't change what had happened at the rock reef, or on my mom's bike ride. I couldn't change anything that already happened. But it was hard to shake the feeling that both accidents were my fault.

CHAPTER 25

FOR TWO more days, it rained. My wound still ran pink. I worked on a new song.

Where does the deer end?
And where do I begin?
Deer flesh in my veins.
I have no hunger pains.

The deer is in my blood.
Blood that feeds my brain.
I couldn't even think a thought.
If that deer had not remained.

I looked it in the eye.
Beauty staring back at me.
I didn't want to kill it.
But then where would I be?

That deer was gonna die.
Its legs were busted bad.
If I didn't take its life.
A big old bear would have.

As I sang, I dried more deer meat. I now had about sixty pieces. My whole life consisted of collecting wood, drying deer meat and eating boiled deer. And thinking. I mean, sometimes my mind was just blank, focused on the task, but other times, when I wasn't singing, it ran and ran.

Last year, Mr. Haskins put a world map on the classroom wall. Then he walked around with a shoe box and we each took three slips of paper. "Find out where the items are grown or produced," Mr. Haskins said. "Then we'll put them on the map."

In Fairbanks I ate bananas from Mexico, drank OJ from Florida, and ate apples from Washington. Everything was shipped in.

But now, I got to thinking about Bear Island.

Everything I ate came from the island. Bear Island deer. Bear Island salmon. Bear Island blueberries. Bear Island porcupine.

And most everything I used, too. Bear Island water. Bear Island boughs for my bed. Bear Island deadfall for my house. Bear Island alder for my grill. Bear Island wood for my spear. Bear Island deerskin for my gloves.

I totally relied on Bear Island.

And I thought about people that lived before ships and planes, those people relied on their places, too. They ate the place, drank the place, breathed the place they lived.

And sure, maybe some people still lived like that, but I didn't think there were too many. Right now, I was one of those people. Yeah, I had my clothes and the few things from the emergency kits, but the longer I stayed, the more I was becoming a Bear Islander. The only Bear Islander that I knew of.

Three more days passed and still it rained. I told myself I'd leave Deer Camp—yeah, that's what I'd named it—as soon as the rain let up—one last push for the Sentinels. I could've left in the rain but didn't want to leave the fire, trade my warm camp for the cold, wet, forest.

A camp with food.

If I hadn't killed the deer, no way would I be staying here. This place was defined by that deer. I'd just keep eating it until the rain stopped, keep singing its song. It'd only make me stronger.

And it was defined by my dad. This was the last place we'd camped together. Somehow, some part of him was here with me. It didn't matter if he was at the Sentinels, or down the coast a ways, or at the bottom of the ocean, I could feel him here too. He was in the air I breathed and the water I drank.

And the bowl? Maybe it really was a gift from my mom. I didn't know what to believe.

It was pretty amazing that I'd lived at Fish Camp, and now at Deer Camp, for almost forty days. Just that I was alive was amazing. But the longer I stayed alive, the more I wanted to survive and make it out of this mess. You know, keep living my life, whatever that life might look like. Any life was better than no life.

I kept gathering wood and drying it out by the fire so it would burn better, but my supply still ran low. One more night I told myself, and then rain or no rain, I'd leave at first light, and go, go, go until dark, and hopefully not hurt myself on the journey. That was one thing about staying put. At least I knew what was around me. And a solid shelter with a fire was like a security blanket. Just like Fish Camp, I knew I had to leave but didn't want to.

I pulled branches from a tangle of deadfall. And carried an armload the hundred yards or so to my shelter. Maybe I could get by with just one more load.

I slogged back to the deadfall and pulled more branches. I was about halfway back with another armload when I saw my shelter bulge and shake.

I stopped walking. My first thought was 'earthquake' followed by 'tsunami,' but the ground wasn't shaking under my feet.

I'd missed an earthquake in Fairbanks once when I was riding my bike on the one flat spot on our driveway. I noticed the leaves shaking in the trees above me and thought it was weird that there was a breeze up there and nothing down on the ground. When I went inside, my mom was freaked out. Turns out it was the biggest earthquake in Fairbanks in fifteen years and I hadn't even felt it. Maybe the driveway was just bumpy. I don't know. We get lots of small quakes that you only feel if you're inside and the house shakes.

And I hadn't felt any earthquakes since I'd been out here.

The summer before my mom died we were on a camping trip and were all lying in the tent, and there was an earthquake. I don't even know how big it was, but I remember it shaking my whole body, like it had gotten under my skin and started vibrating in my bones. Maybe the more of you touching the ground, the more likely you are to feel it. If it just comes through your feet and you're walking, then you miss a lot of it.

At least if an earthquake destroyed my shelter while I was inside it, I'd live. Having a bunch of sticks and branches fall on you would suck, and maybe you'd get scratched up, but it's not like falling glass and crumbling walls.

Out here if there's a big earthquake, then you've gotta head to high ground to avoid a tsunami, you know, a huge wave that basically destroys everything. The tsunami that followed the 1964 Earthquake destroyed a few villages and towns on the coast, and in some places the ground fell by thirty-five feet. Maybe that rock reef that I didn't see in time used to tower out of the water.

Some more boughs and branches fell, creating a hole in my shelter, and I still didn't feel anything. Maybe the shelter was just falling apart. Maybe one of the main deadfall supports had finally broken after all that sagging. Oh well, I could figure it out for one more night. Maybe move the fire inward and hunker down in the back part. I could even burn the extra shelter wood to stay warm. I laughed. I could burn the whole thing little by little and have nothing left by morning.

But then I glimpsed something dark through the hole. I thought it was the tree trunk until it moved. Then more sticks fell, creating a huge hole.

"No!" I screamed. "No!"

CHAPTER 26

THE BEAR had its back to me. I dropped my load of sticks.

My deer. My deer. The bear was crouched over it. I picked up a big stick and hurled it at the bear, hitting it right in the back, but the brute didn't even turn around.

"Hey bear!" I yelled.

It turned its head. I threw another stick, hit it in the shoulder, and it let out a growl. I took a step back. It was bigger and more rounded than the other bears I'd seen.

The bear turned back to the deer, its neck flexing as it tugged. I wished it'd just take the deer and leave. All I wanted was my stuff, my jerky, and I'd hike in the rain right now.

I kept yelling, but it was focused on the deer and didn't seem to care. I ran to the stream, grabbed some rocks, came back and started throwing them. One connected on the back of its head and it turned and growled again. I didn't know if I should keep on throwing or not. I mean, I didn't have a fire to stand behind. I had nothing. Not even my spear.

"Go on," I yelled. "Get!"

But all the bear did was turn back to the deer. I hit it with another rock. Then another. And kept yelling.

The bear started dragging the deer, and the rest of my shelter tumbled to the ground. Then the bear lifted its head and carried the carcass off.

I watched the bear fade into the forest, then approached what used to be my shelter. Sticks and boughs and limbs lay in a pile. Smoke rose through a bunch of spruce boughs on top of the coals in my fire ring.

From the wreckage, I pulled my bowl, two life vests, two emergency blankets, one of which had a large tear down the center, and my spear and gaff.

And the dried deer meat? I found just seven pieces spread among the boughs and sticks. How it hadn't sucked those down with the other fifty-odd pieces I didn't know.

My head drooped. My shoulders collapsed forward as I sat down against the tree. Tears streamed down my cheeks. My chest was hollow, like I'd been opened up with a knife.

I wished I could go back in time, so I could've lugged the jerky around with me. But I didn't want the jerky exposed to the rain, and I hadn't seen any bears, not even any bear sign at this camp, and I had a fire going, and I was never even out of sight of the shelter. How much more careful could I get?

But if I could just have those few minutes back again.

Get sad. Get mad. But move on, Tom. Move on.

I took one of the knives out of my pocket, opened it and thrust the blade into the ground. I pulled it out and then stabbed the Earth again and again.

I just wanted to be dead already.

It was my fault that I was here. My fault that my dad wasn't. My fault that my mom died. My fault that I'd lost my deer meat. My fault.

The cold seeped in. My fingers turned to ice. My arms shook. But still, I just sat against the tree. And even with all the deer I'd eaten these past days, I felt weak, like I hadn't eaten in over a month.

━━

I put a piece of jerky in the bowl and boiled it to make broth. It tasted weak compared to broth made from boiling fresh meat.

I fed the fire and the wind blew smoke into my face and stung my eyes. Then I thought:

> 2 knives
> 1/4 of a fire starter stick
> 7 matches
> 1 lighter
> 1 fishing lure unused and one on the gaff
> 1 bundle of fishing line

4 small pieces of rope
2 small pieces of flint
2 Meal Pack bars that I refused to eat
6 pieces of jerky
This was it—all of it.

CHAPTER 27

THREE DAYS later and I was picking my way along a jagged coast. Fallen columns of black rock jutted into the water every couple hundred yards. The hiss of waves smashing, retreating, and forcing their way between the rocky teeth sounded like static from an untuned radio turned up full blast.

The constant drizzle made it so I was never dry. A pale outline of the sun, masked by gray clouds, hung low in the southern sky. And there was less and less daylight every day.

I'd hoped to kill something, anything, but all I'd seen were sea otters floating on their backs and diving for food, dozens of them. Some with this year's young riding on their chests. I couldn't get close enough to them to even try for a kill. I found a few shriveled berries here and there, clinging to mostly bare branches.

A tiny wail invaded my ears. Like a cross between a crying baby and a whining puppy. Then a louder, deeper call. Then the tiny wail. Then both of them at once. I turned toward where I thought the sound was coming from. The rounded head of a sea otter bobbed in the waves as it swam back and forth close to one of the black rocky points of the coastline.

I saw it open its mouth, heard the deep cry, and then from somewhere, a softer cry. The otter kept swimming back and forth. An eagle flew low over the point and the otter went crazy, continually screaming. I caught snatches of the softer wail, too. The eagle circled back and the otter screamed louder.

My mind ran with ideas. Most of the otters along this stretch had babies riding on their chests.

Two cries.

A loud one and a soft one.

I could see one otter.

A Bald Eagle circling.

I took a breath. A baby otter. This had to have something to do with a baby.

My stomach jumped into my brain and said, "Go see. Go see. Food. This could be food."

I set my gaff and bowl above the strand line, and with my spear in hand, started to work my way out onto the black rocks. My stomach said, "Hurry, you fool. Before the eagle swoops in." But the rock formation was a deadly combination of slippery and sharp.

I used my hands for stability, thankful for the deerskin protecting my fingers. The water was hissing on three sides of me as I approached the end of the point. The otter looked larger now that I could see it up close. Its coal black nose, shaped like a heart, sat in the middle of a rounded gray face between two small black eyes.

It opened its mouth and let out a series of prolonged cries. And from somewhere out of sight, I heard a softer cry in response. I took a breath, then crawled forward on the slick rock, the cold pressing into my chest and empty belly through my clothing. The otter continued to cry. The eagle was circling but hadn't swooped down since I'd been out on the end of the point, but sea gulls were starting to circle too.

Food drives everything, I thought. If you don't go after a meal when it presents itself, then something else will get it. And you had to weigh the danger.

I mean, the eagle had backed off, probably because of me. Had it known I'd gotten my butt kicked by a swan, maybe it would have challenged me. And the gulls were just in it for the scraps. They didn't care who did the killing as long as they got to clean up afterward.

I inched forward, my heart pounding against the black rock. At the very edge I peered down, and on a little ledge I saw it. Crammed between two sharp black teeth, letting out a soft wail, was a smaller version of the crying otter just off shore. It had the same plump heart shaped nose and black eyes, but its fur was light brown instead of gray.

A wave touched the ledge, briefly covering the baby otter, but then it was back in full view, wailing.

My stomach did a little dance. Meat. All that meat. And since the eagle had backed off, that made me the top predator. The only thing I needed to watch out for was the waves. The mother otter was still screaming, and the baby was answering her over and over like a recorded message stuck on replay.

The ledge was about ten feet below me and now that I was ready to climb down I noticed how steep it was. I paused.

Is the payoff worth the risk? There are consequences for trying and consequences for not trying.

There were bumps in the drop that I could use for hand and foot holds but everything was damp and the rocky surface below looked even sharper, and that made me think of my mom.

I watched another wave gently wash over the baby otter. I dropped my spear over the edge, then I swung a leg over and started climbing down with my back to the water, my chest, stomach and the front of my thighs pressing into the slippery rock. One of my feet slipped off the surface and I dug my fingers into the rock as my foot searched for a stable spot. Both my hands slid downward and one of my elbows caught on a bump so I anchored myself there, jammed my foot into a crevice and then kept inching my way down until I was standing on the sharp rocks.

I turned, picked up my spear and faced the water. The mother otter was screaming, the baby answering her while the waves pushed up to the edge of the ledge and retreated. The baby otter was trapped in the bottom of a steep V in the rocks toward the edge of the ledge.

I took a breath and moved toward the otter. The mother out in the water moved in closer to the rocks and just kept on screaming. My eyes met hers and I felt a twinge in the back of my throat. I glanced over at the baby and felt another twinge. It was moving its head up and down but it was clearly stuck or else it would've scrambled out of there.

Twenty or thirty gulls were circling overhead, their calls growing louder the closer I got to the otter. I took a couple of slippery steps toward the baby otter, our eyes met and a lump formed in my throat. I swallowed it down and took another step. It let out a wail, which its mother answered. A wave washed over my boots and the mother otter's gray head appeared inches away, screaming.

I felt the weight of the spear in my hands. The spear I'd used to kill a small porcupine, and then a small deer.

The wave washed back, carrying the mother otter out with it. I watched as she swam back toward me. Then she raised her body up like she was standing on something, and her face, for just an instant, was replaced by my mom's. I blinked and stared at the otter and for an instant I saw my mom's face again.

I turned my eyes toward the baby who now lay silent, its chest moving up and down rapidly. I squatted and touched one of its rubbery webbed feet. It leaned its head forward and let out a small whine. My stomach grumbled and my heart ached as the mother's cries continually filled my ears.

I pulled on the foot and its whole body moved about an inch then stopped. I grabbed its other foot and turned the otter sideways. It let out a few more whines but I couldn't see its face because it was pressed against the rock.

Its thick tail hung limp between its webbed feet like it'd given up. Like it was offering itself to me. But the mother was still screaming. I pulled the pup toward me, hoping I wasn't causing it pain by being dragged through the V in the rocks but there was no other way to remove it.

A wave washed over the ledge and cold water poured into my boots, and the otter pup's body strained against being sucked back into the V.

"Easy," I said to the pup. "Easy." My stomach burned. And my throat ached. And my hands were going numb even though my arms were sweating.

Do what you think is right. Do what is true to you.

The mother otter's screams were bouncing around in my head. Another tug and the baby would be completely out of the V and in my control. I glanced at my spear which was pinned underneath my boots, glad that I'd had the forethought to secure it or else the waves would have taken it.

"Okay, little guy," I said. "Here we go." Before I pulled I turned toward the mother and looked into her black pain-filled eyes. "Don't worry," I said. "Don't you worry."

In one sweeping motion I swung the pup out of the V and into the water. The mother grabbed her pup and backpedaled away from the black rock, the pup riding on her chest.

I lifted my hand and waved. The mother poked her head forward and up, like maybe she was nodding at me, and then dropped beneath the surface, taking her pup with her.

I plucked my spear off the rocky ledge. My mom's face flashed in my mind. I knew what it was like to be separated from someone you loved. Someone you cared about. I knew the pain of the sudden death of someone close to you.

I saw the otters surface in the distance and I felt a small smile form on my face. My stomach was still empty but my heart was full.

———

Late in the day, I climbed to the top of a headland and stopped to rest. A few blue spots dotting the wall of clouds gave me hope that I'd get another break from the rain and wet. Not that it mattered what the weather would be like when I died. In my mind I pictured that sea otter pup. All the meat I had in my hands, and said, "No, I did the right thing." My mom's face, smiling, invaded my brain. She was nodding her head and there were tears on her cheeks.

I pulled out my last piece of jerky. I was gonna save it for the night and boil it, but I was hungry now.

I looked at the steep slope as I chewed, trying to pick the easiest route down.

The coast bent back. The inlet with the copper-colored cliffs. Huge cliffs, I remembered. I let out a breath. Another piece of water to walk around. Something you could cross in a kayak in thirty minutes. I wished I could walk on water. We'd camped in the back of this inlet. It had a narrow entrance, but the water wound back for a few miles through steep country. Sheer cliffs rising from the water one thousand feet or more in lots of places. Hard-walking country.

I thought about the lakes above Hidden Bay. Was that pass a short cut to the Sentinels? Would I already be there if I'd gone that way? I thought about the prints I'd seen on the lakeshore. Had my dad gone that way?

Choices. Life was full of choices. Don't look back, I told myself. It does no good. I swallowed the last of my jerky and started down the slope in search of a place to camp.

CHAPTER 28

IN THE morning, I didn't want to move out from under the spruce boughs I'd piled up, then crawled into. Didn't want to face the day with no food. But through the web of needles and branches, I saw the sun poking some rays into the ravine I'd camped in, and I couldn't waste that.

I sat up and pushed through the boughs like I was hatching from an egg. I stretched my arms, then closed my eyes to keep the sun out. I fell back onto the boughs, but the north wind bending into the inlet chilled me, telling me to get up and get going.

I squatted by the trickle of water that flowed through the ravine, filled my bowl and drank, willing my body to live off the water.

I tied my pile jacket around my middle, knowing I'd soon be warm from climbing to the crest of the cliffs on the opposite side of the ravine. Or at least attempting to climb. Food or no food, as long as I could still move, I'd keep going.

And I thought it was crazy that I'd survived even this long. Figuring out how to catch fish, build shelters, dry meat. And how to do all that without going crazy, or shriveling up in fear, or sinking into a pit of depression, or when I did sink, being able to haul myself out. And despite all the mistakes I'd made, I was still here. Still walking toward the Sentinels.

I laughed a sad laugh. I guess I'd survived so far by just paying attention and not giving up. And the mistakes, yeah, I'd made a bunch, but I'd kept going. I thought about the sea otter pup and about all that meat, and said out loud, "That wasn't a mistake. That was a choice."

And not going crazy from being alone? I still didn't know what to think about that. Why wasn't I a nutcase by now? Maybe I was, and just couldn't tell.

I climbed to the crest of the first cliff. I could see across the inlet to the copper-colored cliffs on the other side and knew I was standing on the same. And back from the cliffs, the mountains rose, fresh snow on the peaks.

On the flat-topped ridge, giant evergreens towered over me while the wind pushed me along. I wished all the walking was this easy. Just a stroll through flat, open forest all the way to the Sentinels. And when I made it, there'd be a boat, and people, and food, lots of food. Candy bars, chips, steak.

I climbed up and down three more times, my legs weak from lack of food somehow still moving forward.

Take two steps and rest. Two steps and rest. That's how I got myself up that final ridge.

I could hear a stream now, somewhere below me, running through a fold in the copper cliffs.

Down there. Where I'd camped with Dad. Down there somewhere. When we still had the kayak. When we were on an adventure together.

"Just me now," I said. "Me and the wild. I'm wild. Part of the wild."

I even felt like I belonged on Bear Island. Not belonged like I should stay here forever, but belonged like I was part of the place. And that feeling of belonging, I realized, had helped me to keep going.

I was living in the place, getting all I needed from it to keep my heart ticking and lungs sucking.

Sure, I still wanted some chicken enchiladas and salsa and Coke and some chocolate cake. I wanted a hot shower. And to read my mom's stories and listen to her music, and to play her guitar. And to meet up with Heather if she moved back to Fairbanks. I wanted to help my dad set up the wall tent and walk his snowshoe trails with him.

But on Bear Island all I wanted was food and warmth. And to not be eaten. Without those, all my other wants were meaningless.

I picked my way along the spine of the ridge and then started down. The mouth of the creek came into view. The fresh water fanned out into three main channels, the cliffs folding back on themselves, giving the stream room to enter the inlet. Islands of pale yellow seaweed and black rock separated the channels. Sea gulls worked the islands, pecking and squawking and flapping their wings in the sun that was soon to disappear over the ridge. A speck of water rose in the channel closest to me.

Late run. Late run of Silvers. Is that what Dad had said? I tried to remember, but my mind, like my body, was tired, depleted, like a balloon left out in the cold that had lost most of its air. I reached deeper, trying to recall, willing the memory to the surface, willing his voice to speak, but came up empty. Maybe a late run of silver salmon, that's all I could remember. Maybe it was the same with that first creek in Hidden Bay where I thought I'd find fish, or maybe they both didn't have any salmon, period.

I worked my way downslope, pausing several times to scan the mouth of the creek, thankful that I'd had the couple of weeks with Dad out here. Maybe he was at the Sentinels, waiting. Something was, I could feel it.

I hoped and wished that someday, somehow, my dad could know all I'd done out here. Even if I died tonight, I wanted Dad to know that I was dredging up every memory I could, every word of his wisdom, big and small alike. And that every time I heard his voice was a gift. If he survived and I didn't, could I send him a message? Could I be a voice in his head?

Down in the thigh-high beach grass I made noise. "Hey Bear! Hey Bear! Hey Bear!" I almost stepped on the first salmon carcass before I saw it. A shriveled head, no eyes, a long backbone with a little dried skin on the tail. Bigger than the pink salmon from Fish Camp.

Closer to the creek I found two more carcasses, but they were too nasty to even think about eating. Then I found a pile of bear scat.

I poked it with a stick. Dry on top and gooey underneath.

Day old. Maybe two, I guessed. My dad was always poking scat. Always trying to figure out exactly when it'd been ejected from some animal's rear and what it contained. My mom would occasionally humor him and pretend to be interested but if my dad carried on for too long, she'd just look at him with this face that said, "Okay, I know you're interested in this, but maybe you could tone it down a little." Or, "Just think about it but don't tell me every little detail."

At first I didn't see the dark forms that blended with the rocks of the creek bottom. Not until they moved. Half a dozen salmon held steady in the current.

Fish. Fresh fish. Not as many as the pinks at Fish Camp, but at least there was some.

I stopped myself from trying the gaff in the deep water, and walked along the channel upstream in search of a shallow spot. At the edge of the forest, where the three braids came together, the water was still deep, three feet or more. I noticed two more groups of fish resting on the bottom of the channel.

I paused and took a deep breath. I wanted those fish. Needed those fish to fill out my caved-in stomach. To nourish the army of starved cells that made up my body. In my mind I willed the salmon to the surface so I could gaff them. And eat them. But they didn't respond.

In the forest, the creek spilled over boulders and fallen logs, the rush of flowing water filling my ears. The water echoed off the canyon walls which were set back a few hundred feet from the creek. And the trees hugged the channel, closing it in so you couldn't see upstream for more than a couple hundred feet at a stretch. At one point a large tree had fallen across the creek, spanning the thirty-foot width.

I straddled the log instead of standing on it, knowing that a fall leading to an injury, any injury, could be the end for me. I scooted my way across, like I was playing leap-frog. I walked downstream, light-headed but alert.

Fish.

Fish.

Fish.

"Hey bear. Hey bear," I called out of habit.

Once out of the forest, I followed the channel into the intertidal zone at the edge of the beach grass.

Two more nasty carcasses.

Then I observed several large dark shadows move sideways and away from me in the shallowest water I'd seen. I froze, and then took one step backwards, my head pointing straight with my eyes straining to the side and downwards, studying the fish. I took two more slow steps backwards.

I untied my pile jacket and Dad's raincoat, let them fall with the life vests in the beach grass next to my gaff, spear, and bowl. I picked up the gaff, and glanced back and forth between it and the creek. Still too deep. I set it down and palmed the spear. Again I looked from the spear to the creek and back several times.

I edged toward the water, my spear cupped in both hands. Three fish rested on the bottom of the channel. I focused on the fish closest to me. When I knelt, the pointy edges of the broken rock bit into my knees, like thumbtacks.

I sucked in a breath and held it, then raised the spear over my head. I aimed for the center of the closest fish, thrust the spear downwards and caught the fish just beneath the gills.

"Yes! Yes! Yes!" I shouted.

The fish flapped madly. I tried to lift it, but my spear came up empty, and the wounded fish escaped upstream. A deserted stretch of water lay beneath me.

A quiver ran through my body.

"Okay, fish. I'll find you." I said, while staring at the stream. "I will search. Search. And search. And I'll just keep on searching."

Search.

Search.

Search. The word played over in my mind as I pounded upstream. But I found nothing. So I turned toward the forest in search of a campsite. Precious daylight was fading.

THE ACCIDENT

I let go of my paddle, pushed free of the cockpit, and cleared the surface, sucking air in rapid-fire breaths like I'd just run a marathon. I reached for the nose of the capsized kayak, trying to claw my way out of the cold that was surrounding me—squeezing me like a giant hand.

But another wave pummeled the kayak, jerked it from my grip, and pushed me under.

I broke the surface and heard a series of cracks, and a crazy screeching sound, but my hood was plastered onto my head so I couldn't see anything but the green and white of the water. I was kicking my legs and trying to catch my breath. And Dad, where was he?

I yanked my hood back and kept kicking.

CHAPTER 29

THE NEXT morning I kicked at the dead fire, gathered my stuff and headed for the creek. I'd spent the night with my back to a big tree and a fire in my face, wishing I had a fish.

The sun poured through a notch in the headland to the south, spilling long, narrow rays on the water at the mouth of the creek. The tide was coming in. I needed food, and this was my chance.

I'd thought some about the spear last night and realized I had to do more than puncture the fish. I needed a way for the spear to take hold so the fish wouldn't slip off. And then, I had a thought—a hook. Place a hook close to the end of the spear. So I took the hook off the gaff and attached it to the spear with fishing line and rope an inch or two from the end.

Now, a group of salmon swayed in the water just upstream from where I was standing. I stepped back from the bank, then moved upstream about thirty feet.

One baby step at a time, I crept toward the creek.

The fish held steady in the current. I gripped my spear with both hands, aimed for the closest fish, and thrust down. I caught the silver salmon mid-way between the gills and the dorsal fin. It tried to pull me across the channel, but I raised my spear up and out at the same time and scrambled away from the bank, the big fish swimming in the air.

I dropped the spear in the beach grass, with the flopping fish still attached to it, picked up a rock and clubbed the Silver Salmon. Still, it flopped.

I grabbed it by the tail, then smacked it on the head again. Its eyes bulged from the sockets. I wanted to tear into that fish, eat it raw, eyeballs and brains and all, but knew I needed to catch as many as I could. I took my knife out and made a few slits around the hook and worked it out of the fish.

I turned toward the creek, but then remembered the bear scat I'd seen yesterday. So I spun a slow circle, listening, looking and feeling my surroundings, then examined the spear. The hook had slid forward a little so I slid it back and retightened the ropes and line. Then I faced the creek again.

———

Six fish, gutted, lay on the beach grass. My shirt stuck to my body from sweat, but my hands were numb. I'd retightened the ropes and line each time I'd speared a fish.

The morning was gone, the sun already starting its descent. And high clouds from the south were reaching over the cove, promising rain.

Grasping the fish at the base of their tails, I carried them two at a time into the forest where I'd picked out a spot for my shelter.

Two small trees had fallen, one on top of the other, making an X. The crown of the bottom tree rested in the crook of a standing tree. The second tree rested crosswise on the first. The middle of the X was about as tall as me.

I covered the space between the fallen trees from where they crossed down to their root wads with branches and boughs, a distance of about seven feet.

I wanted to keep working on my shelter, but the clouds were really piling up so I switched to collecting firewood. Then I hauled rocks from the creek—enough for two fire rings in front of the shelter—and got a fire going.

Again I was able to push myself even though I'd eaten almost nothing the past few days—like the day I'd killed the deer. I had some food coming, so my mind pushed my starved body and my body responded, like the energy came from a bottomless well when I knew I had food coming.

Mind power. Push. Push. Push.

And this time I hadn't even hurt myself with my spear. The lump on the side of my head was gone. The wound under my jaw was still sore, but it'd stopped leaking pink fluid. And the swan bite was a memory. Just a thin, raised line below my ear lobe.

I put the eggs from three salmon in the bowl with water, along with a couple of thick salmon steaks. The rest of the cut fish, along with the other five, I moved from outside to inside.

I ended up eating three bowls of fish and broth. My stomach bulged like I'd swallowed a volleyball. I guess that was because I was so freaking skinny.

If only it could be like this all the time. Not the skinny part, but having warm food, a simple shelter, and a fire.

If only that creek always had fish in it, and the forest was full of berries year-round.

But it wasn't like that. Life cycled. Seasons changed. I felt like I belonged, but at the same time knew that I was just passing through.

Some animals lived in one area their whole lives, not the salmon and not the bears. When the fish weren't running, the bears had to find food somewhere else, just like me. And in the winter, they hibernated.

I guess I'd either get lucky and be rescued, or not. But the one thing I had control over was trying to stay alive. I mean, what if I gave up and someone found me the day after I died?

And even if I died out here, I'd rather live as many days as I could. It was my life, and if I had to choose between two weeks or three, or ten days or twelve, I'd take the bigger number every time, even if I was starving or hurt and in pain. I bet my mom would've taken another day or even another hour if she'd had the chance. And my dad, maybe he'd reached the Sentinels, a boat had come and this very minute they were motoring up the coast searching for me. And if I just gave up, they'd find me dead instead of alive.

In the morning, one of my fires still had some coals, which was good because I only had four matches left, and I didn't know how long the lighter would last. And I still hadn't tried starting a fire with the flint.

I rekindled the fire, and added larger pieces of wood until the flames were knee high. Then I grabbed the bowl and jogged to the creek. The tide was way out.

Some branches, barely waving, caught my eye. I peered across the creek into the forest, blinked my eyes and squinted.

Bear. Was it a bear? It was something. I'd felt something.

Something watching me.

My stomach tightened. My heart thumped. Bear. Bear. Bear.

"Hey bear," I called. "I know you're over there."

I glanced over my shoulder several times as I beat it back to my shelter.

I'm sick of this crap. Not only do I have to worry about having enough to eat, I've got to worry about being eaten.

Instead of wishing things were different, put your energy into the current situation.

"Shut up! Just shut up!" I tried to block my dad's voice from my mind, even though deep down I knew his words rang true.

But sometimes you didn't want to hear the truth. You just wanted someone to swoop down and take care of you. Someone to step in and make it all right. Someone you trusted who'd say, "You'll be okay, just come with me." Or, "You just relax, you've done a great job. I'll take it from here."

I knew I had to take care of myself. That no one was going to do anything for me. And when it comes right down to it, you have to rely on yourself. You've got to live with yourself and the choices you make.

Like after Mom died and Dad disappeared inside himself, I felt so guilty for not going on that bike ride that I just disappeared too.

I managed to get through school. But I still had to live with myself, just like I was now with the memory of my mistake that caused the kayak accident. It wasn't an easy life, but it was my only life.

I placed the bowl of water with a thick hunk of salmon in it on the smoothed-out bed of coals, then gathered wood.

I covered my shelter with more and more boughs and it took on a rounded shape, like the Earth had burped a bough-bubble and I'd cut out an entrance for a door. Like it was a hatch leading underground. Between the two fire rings at the entrance, I stacked firewood and covered it with a layer of boughs.

Just inside the shelter on the right I put a pile of throwing stones and behind the stones, more firewood. On the left side I stacked more firewood, leaving just enough space to lie down on the life vests.

Then a storm blew in that night.

CHAPTER 30

COLD RAIN fell for three days. The woods turned soggy. Water everywhere. Wind came and went in gusts. The torn pieces of emergency blanket I'd managed to tack up over my sleeping area reflected some of the light and warmth from the fires and kept most of the rain off of me. The rest of the shelter was much drier than outside, but in time water found its way in through the boughs and dripped.

My old friends RF and LF tried to cheer me up. They popped, sizzled, cracked and smoked in protest every time I put a piece of soggy wood on top of their coals.

"Without us," RF said, "you'd be screwed."

"That's no joke," LF added.

"Yeah," I said. "But without me, you wouldn't even exist. You were just some random pieces of dead wood until I came along."

"Well, Master Fire-maker," RF said. "You better conquer that flint. I saw your match supply. We don't just spontaneously burst into flames."

LF agreed. "Learn how to use it before you need it."

Then they both just sat there, burning away, waiting for me to try.

I pulled the flint out of the ziplock bag. At home, dad collected lint from the dryer and kept it in a plastic bag, and he'd bring some of it to the wall tent. The first time he showed me how a knife and a piece of flint could start a fire he'd rained sparks on a little nest of dryer lint. It caught and burned, the blue lint putting off a black smoke. I was maybe seven-years-old. He didn't want me playing with a sharp knife so he gave me a thin piece of metal and I practiced making sparks. My sparks weren't as big as his, and I couldn't make as many of them, and my piece of dryer lint just sat there like it was covered with some kind of fire-proof layer. But I kept working at it and later that winter, I finally got some flames.

Next, Dad showed me how a nest of crushed up birch bark and dried grass could be coaxed into burning.

But out here, in this soggy piece of forest, nothing was dry. Nothing. I sighed and sat back.

"Dude," LF said. "I don't think it works that way."

"Yeah," said RF. "It's not magic."

"Just pick it up and try," LF said. "What else are you going to do during this storm?"

"Okay," I nodded. I pulled a piece of wood from the pile, grabbed my knife, sat cross legged right in front of LF, and started whittling the thinnest shavings I could. The knife skipped on knots and often dug deeper than I wanted it to, but I kept at it, stopping only to stoke RF and LF.

After I'd made a pretty sizeable pile, I set my knife down and cupped the shavings into my hands like I was making a snowball.

Dryer lint, I thought. This ball of shavings looks nothing like a nest of dryer lint. I rose up on my knees, grabbed the flint and held it so the tip was touching the shavings. I took my knife and ran the blade down the flint and a large spark dropped off which was immediately swallowed by the shavings. I ran the knife up and down the flint creating a storm of sparks which all died quick deaths in the pile of shavings.

I took a breath and rained more sparks down and saw a tiny bit of red and then one puff of smoke coming from the end of a very thin shaving, but then it was gone. The fatter shavings just sat there, spark proof.

I set the flint down and swept the shavings into RF and they curled, then burst into flames. I could feel the heat building behind my eyes.

"Poor baby," RF said. "Couldn't start a fire."

"He barely tried," LF chimed in.

"Shut up. Both of you," I said. "I spent a couple hours making those shavings."

"And you just quit?" RF said. "You have four matches left. Some or all of those might be duds."

"I don't care," I said. "If I can't do it, I can't do it. You can't say I didn't try."

"You call that trying?" LF said. "When you first tried to catch a salmon and didn't, did you just give up?"

"Okay," I said softly. "I get it. I'm not stupid."

The smoke, I thought. The smoke came from a very thin shaving. I grabbed another piece of firewood, rose up on my knees and leaned forward so one end of the wood pressed against my stomach and the other end was on the ground like I was a little kid playing airplane with my dad, the piece of wood replacing his feet.

I picked up my knife and ran it along the wood, working the rough bark off one side in thick pieces. Then I started running the knife at an angle to the flat surface I'd created, letting the blade barely connect with the wood.

"Thin," I said to my knife. "Make them thin. Ultra thin. See-through thin."

But the knife kept wanting to go deeper and deeper, like it was preprogrammed to do so, but I wanted it shallow, to barely touch the surface and to do it at an angle, to catch a raised spot and run with it. Long, thin, curly shavings, like confetti, that's what I was after.

After what seemed like forever, I sat back to take a rest. To stretch my hands which had started cramping up.

LF popped once, then said, "Pretty good start, but you'll need more."

I separated the thin, curly shavings from the thick, flat ones, and stared at a mound smaller than a golf ball.

The rain continued to fall. I put more wood on RF and LF and then lay down on the life vests. Making fire-making materials was work. Hard work.

Dryer lint, I thought. As close to dryer lint as possible. I thought about the four matches and hoped they weren't all duds. The thin shavings would catch with a match but with the flint, I just didn't know. I mean, if it took hours to make the shavings and they didn't work, then what? What would I do?

I kneeled in front of the tiny pile of shavings and threw shower after shower of sparks onto them. I saw a little red glow and then smoke. I rained more sparks and saw more red dots and more smoke. I stopped and blew gently on the shavings, the red glow increased but no flames shot up. I rained more sparks down, got more red glows, blew again, but still no flame.

I pushed the shavings into RF and they immediately burst into flame.

"Okay," I said. "I'm closer than I was." But the problem gnawed at my brain like a starving beaver with worn-out teeth working the base of a birch tree.

The rain let up on the fourth day. Worry over food and firewood consumed my thoughts. I had enough wood for a couple of days if I rationed it, and one fish. I'd kept working at the flint and so far all I could get was red glow and smoke. I thought maybe there was some step I was missing. If only I could see it in my mind. I'd asked dad, hoping his voice would boom out the answer but had been met with silence. RF and LF hadn't been much help either. You'd think they'd know since they're fires but all they did was tell me to shut up and keep trying.

At the shore my stomach clenched when I saw the continuous white blanket in the high country. Snow had fallen and accumulated up there while it had rained at sea level. And the snow line was lower than I'd seen it. I hoped it wouldn't get any lower, but I knew winter was closing in. I could feel it in the stillness, like the snow had put a lid on the island. The hammer was coming down.

I scanned the swelled creek for fish all up and down the tidal part but came up empty, so I headed upstream into the forest.

A splash made my heart jump. I saw the black rump disappearing ahead of me. But I kept going upstream. Bear or no bear, I needed fish.

I rounded a few bends, yelling "hey bear," then I saw what I was hoping to see. Fish. Their noses were white. And there were white splotches at the bases of their fins. Kind of sick-looking, but they were still alive. I counted—eleven fish. I wanted them all. I pulled cold air through my nose and felt a chill crawl up my spine.

The pool was about ten feet across, six feet long, with a four-foot waterfall spilling into it. I choked up on the spear and slipped into the water opposite the waterfall, trying to create as little disturbance as possible.

The school of fish moved upstream toward the waterfall.

I took two more steps. Still out of reach. I needed another foot or two to get a good shot.

My chest felt hollow, like it'd been scooped out with a big spoon. If I didn't get these fish, I was history.

I advanced on the fish, and sucked air as the creek filled my boots and tugged at my thighs. Raising the spear, I took aim and then thrust downward and forward, connecting on a large salmon just below the gills. I lifted the spear and discovered I had thrust the point through the gills and into the fish's mouth.

The fish flapped wildly. I swung the spear toward shore, the fish skimming across the water, and tossed it onto the forest floor. The fish was flopping and the spear was bouncing up and down. I climbed out of the creek, grabbed a rock and clubbed that fish until its eyes bulged. With my knife I slit the side of its mouth and popped the spear out. Then I checked the hook and re-entered the creek.

The rest of the school had scattered, but there were still a bunch of fish in the small pool. I pierced another fish in the white belly tissue, swung it up into the forest next to the first fish, then searched again.

The third fish I found behind me and dangerously close to leaving the pool as most of the other fish had already done. I drove the spear, catching the fish midway between head and tail, heaving it to shore all in one motion. In much the same way, I caught two more fish.

I sat and twisted my boots off, and poured the water out. Then took my heelless socks off, wrung them out and put them back on my red, aching feet, followed by my boots.

With icy hands, I gutted the fish, and ran a rope through their gills to carry them. Five fish, I was soaked. I shivered. Plus one at camp. I'd hoped for more. Could've used more. But six fish is better than none. I shivered again.

CHAPTER 31

THE NEXT day I made a drying rack, woven from thin, green alder branches. It was kind of bumpy, but I hoped it'd get the job done and keep me from having to always be looking for more alder.

I knew the Sentinels couldn't be far. My plan: dry some fish, then go.

I took six sticks, whittled the ends into points, and using a rock for a hammer, drove them into the ground in a circle around RF, so the rack could sit just above the coals without burning up.

I made a mess of filleting the first fish. I'd seen my dad fillet salmon, but he used a long knife with a thin blade, not a squat pocketknife.

And he worked at the kitchen counter or on a table outside, and wore these special gloves that helped him grip the fish. I was squatting over a pad of rounded rocks away from the fire, shivering in damp clothes and working barehanded.

Hunks of orange flesh clung to the backbone and ribs of that first salmon, but I boiled it all up with the head, which actually worked out pretty good because I wanted to save all the dried fish for my trip.

I cut the ragged fillets into thin strips and laid them on the rack, figuring the smaller the pieces the faster they'd dry.

I spread out the coals and put the rack on the stakes. But the heat from RF was inconsistent. Sometimes it flared up, charring the fish, making it crispy. I gnawed on the stubborn pieces stuck to the rack, not letting anything go to waste.

I just kept cutting and drying, cutting and drying, all day and all night. And I kept loading the bowl with fish bones and heads and bits of flesh. I'd boil it up on LF, drink the broth, and pick the bones clean. Get more water from the creek and do it again.

"I'm sick of staring up at this rack," RF said, popping in protest and sending a spray of ash onto the drying filets.

"Get this bowl off my coals before I melt it down," LF said, hissing as water from the bowl ran down the sides and onto the coals.

"Just chill," I said.

"Chill?" RF said.

"Dude," said LF. "We're fires. We don't chill. You're the one that's gonna chill if you don't master that flint."

I'd been working on the "flint problem" in my mind but hadn't tried any of my ideas yet because I'd been working on the fish.

The dried fish I stored in my dad's raincoat, which I kept inside my shelter surrounded and covered with boughs. And every time I put more fish in there I'd think of my dad, and puzzle over how that raincoat appeared so close to Fish Camp. And how the bottom third of it was shredded. Had a bear shredded it or had it been dragged over sharp rocks by the surf? Where had it washed up? And what were the chances that an animal would drag it into the forest and leave it so close to Fish Camp? It was more than a coincidence, I thought.

By morning I'd dried all the fish, so I stoked RF and LF, took the dried fish, and set off for the creek with my spear and knife. I hadn't slept, but didn't feel tired. I guess that nomad part of my brain clicked on and said: "Food! You better get it while you can!"

I stepped onto the beach grass and the frost crinkled under my boots. The wet cliffs, without the sun, were a drab gray.

I peered into the creek channel, searching for movement, for fish. Finding none, I headed upstream, hoping that some fish had returned to the pool under the waterfall.

Below the waterfall four fish rested in the middle of the pool, their snouts hooked, their fins ragged with spotty white skin.

The end of the run, I thought. And hopefully not the end of me.

Nature never loses.

Never.

It didn't matter who died and who survived, the dead were continuously recycled.

Those four fish were valuable to me. Alone, they could keep me going for a little while, but combined with what I already had, they might get me all the way to the Sentinels and then some.

I just had to catch them.

———

I killed three of the four fish, but got soaked to my waist. And the fourth fish stole my hook when the line broke and it somehow powered its way over the small waterfall. I tried to find it upstream, but stopped when the creek turned into a quarter-mile-long lake bordered by thick brush.

Back at my shelter, I built up RF and LF and stripped so I was naked from the waist down. My feet were hunks of frozen meat. I stood on a life vest between LF and RF. My toes, which had turned white, stung as they began to thaw; like a swarm of yellow jackets was attacking them.

I dried my socks and long johns and the insides of my boots as best I could. I pushed through the night drying fish, working on a song.

> I live in the trees by this salmon stream.
> In my house of sticks I dry fish and I dream.
> In my dream I see my dad looking for me.
> Searching, searching, searching, under every tree.
> I hear his loud shout, and I answer back.
> I scream, "Keep coming. You're on the right track."
> He's looking kind of skinny, but he's alive.
> Now we'll go home, and together we'll thrive.

The predawn sky was turning a yellowish gray as I put the final batch of dried salmon into the raincoat. I kept RF and LF going. The heat made me drowsy, but kept me from freezing. I'd be able to sleep tonight, but right now I had work to do.

First, I checked out my stuff. I did that every couple of days. I knew what I had, but I wanted to see it, check for any damage. Plus, these things were my connection to the outside world. They reminded me that I was trying to get off this island, back to civilization. If I didn't get off the island I was toast.

I had one fishhook left. And four matches. A lighter, which I hoped would keep working. The flint pieces, at least I had those, but I had my doubts about starting a fire with them since all I'd gotten was smoke. But I had a little hope too. I mean, there was a time before dryer lint when people started fires.

The knives—they were still in good shape, but if I didn't find fish or some other animals they weren't of much use.

And two Meal Pack bars.

And my clothes. Rain pants torn in several places. My long underwear tops and bottoms had worn out some but didn't have any holes. My gloves appeared to be stable thanks to the strips of deerskin I'd used to repair them. My raincoat, wool cap and pile jacket were in decent condition. But my rubber boots were paper thin at the ankles, and my socks had no heels.

This late in the season with the clothes I had, I needed to keep moving to stay warm unless I was by a fire.

And just like Fish Camp, I didn't want to leave this place—Silver Camp. I just wanted someone to find me here. To come zipping into the cove with a boat and take me out of here. I didn't want to start walking again and have to spend the night shivering or fending off bears, or both. And I didn't want my feet to get all torn up again.

I looked around and took it all in. The back part of the shelter still had dry, small- dimension wood, good for rekindling fires. The bough nest had all that silver salmon, smoked and dried, packed in a raincoat. Behind and to my right, a small pile of bigger sticks lay ready for burning. Directly to my right was a pile of palm-sized throwing stones.

The fire rings. RF with the six stakes. The rack lay off to the side, just outside my shelter. And LF, who had a knee-high blaze radiating heat. Between them lay a pile of firewood covered in boughs.

If I did stay, I could live for maybe two weeks on the fish. Longer if I caught a few more or killed something else. And I could stay pretty dry and warm. But then, what if no one came? The sea otter pup flashed into my mind. If I'd taken it instead of giving it back to its mom, maybe I wouldn't even be here. Maybe that would've been enough meat to get me to the Sentinels. But I had done what I had done. And, I was here. And that mother otter had gotten her baby back.

I used the last of my fishing line to attach the last hook to my spear, and checked the creek from the mouth to the waterfall twice. No sign of fish. I hauled some rocks from the creek and spelled 'Sentinels' in front of my shelter. In the morning, I'd go.

End of the Island. The Sentinels. My only chance. And people might not even be there.

━━━

Just beyond the beds of glowing coals, something lurked. I could feel it.

I swung my left arm, grabbed a stick and fed it to the coals on RF. I did this several times, then scooted forward and blew. Small flames licked the kindling and reached upward. I waited for RF to grow, then sat up. My right hand rested on the pile of throwing stones, my fingers curling around one.

Then I heard it. A snuffing sound. I set down the stone and gripped my spear. Maybe it was another porcupine, another meat meal. With the other hand I fed RF small sticks to increase the light. And then piled a bunch of sticks on LF's coals.

I could hear it breathing, sniffing—probably looking for a meal.

Then I heard a slight scuffing, a scratching noise. All this along with my own heart pounding in my ears like it was trapped and wanted out.

I heard a short grunt. Then a snort. Then another grunt.

The sticks on LF caught, and threw light, and I saw it rubbing its snout on the rock pad where I'd cut up the fish.

But it wasn't a porcupine.

This bear looked thin and ragged compared to the others I'd encountered. Its fur hung off its body the way my clothes hung off mine.

I set down my spear and picked up a throwing stone.

The bear grunted again as it continued to root around, licking the salmon-flavored duff and the flat rocks where I'd cut up the fish. I was gonna yell, but the bear hadn't even paid attention to me. Maybe it would just leave.

I kept adding sticks to both RF and LF.

Minutes passed and it just licked and licked, like a little kid with an ice cream cone. I kept building both fires, the flames were waist high and growing. If I wasn't careful I'd catch the roof on fire.

The bear stopped licking, turned its head toward me, and emitted a long, low growl. I stood up in a half-squat, grabbed the bowl and banged on it with a stick.

"Get!"

The bear came forward and growled again. I pounded on the bowl and yelled. Again the bear pawed forward and growled another long, low growl. It definitely knew about me now. But it was acting strange. It wasn't running, but it wasn't attacking.

I had to let it know that this was my place so I rifled a throwing stone, but missed its head.

The bear grunted, then took another step toward me.

I yelled, "Hey bear," and it just kept coming closer, like my voice was drawing it in, its eyes shining in the firelight. I could've pushed my spear through the fire and poked it but knew I didn't have enough leverage to make a difference, so I just stood my ground behind my fires, my thighs burning from the half-squat position I was holding, waiting.

The bear lowered its head and licked the ground.

I tossed more sticks on both fires.

The bear moved to one side and sniffed. Then it grabbed my alder grill and started chewing on it. I didn't care about the grill, but I wanted this bear out of my face because the next link in the chain of chewable treats was me. Then my dried fish.

I threw another rock, smashing the bear on the shoulder. It dropped the grill and looked up, and I pelted it right between the eyes. The bear let out a sharp scream and turned. Whether my next throw hit the bear's hind end as it was running away, I couldn't tell.

"And stay out!" I yelled.

Sometimes older bears won't find enough food to be able to go into hibernation. Watch out for these, they're the most dangerous.

I added more sticks to LF and RF, my eyes glued to the darkness beyond.

THE ACCIDENT

"Swim for shore!"

I turned toward my dad's distant voice and saw him bobbing with his back to the reef.

"Dad!" I raised my arm.

The back half of the boat was under water and the front half was sinking.

"Dad!"

I started to kick toward him, saw him reach his arm toward me, but another wave pounded me under. I pulled upward with my arms, got my head above the water and turned toward where I'd last seen my dad, but backwash from the rock reef filled my mouth and eyes with salt water. Then another wave forced me under.

CHAPTER 32

I STUMBLED on a slippery rock, and grabbed a tree leaning over the water. Thick clouds were piling up. Dark gray clouds that said, "I'm gonna soak you." The wind stung my face, blowing the first raindrops sideways.

Two days of calm, where I'd made my way southward, were coming to an end. I'd spent last night leaning against a big tree within a semi-circle of fire, keeping the bears and the cold away.

It'd taken me a day to get out of the inlet, and now I was making my way down the open coast, but the walking had been slow, with thick stands of trees to weave through, and way more cliffs than beach.

Now I needed to build another shelter. But I didn't want to put the time and energy into building something I'd only be spending one night in. I just wanted to get to the Sentinels before I ran out of food.

The rain came in cold sheets with the wind backing it. I huddled in a four-foot-wide crevice between two boulders. I'd piled some sticks and boughs over the opening to make a roof, and was hoping the wind wouldn't blow it all onto me. I fed a sputtering fire, then wrapped myself in an emergency blanket. And I'd used the last of my matches.

By crouching over the fire with the blanket partially open, I trapped heat but not enough to keep from shivering. And when I sat back I got even colder. But my legs kept cramping up and I had no choice but to sit back unless I wanted to fall into the fire. So I did this back-and-forth thing for a while. I couldn't stand up because my head would've crashed through the roof.

Smoke kept pouring into my face, but I just squeezed my eyes closed and my mom's lyrics flooded my mind.

Every fire's a ceremony.

Every story's a testimony.

If you pay attention, you will know what the river knows.

All I knew was that I was freezing. I felt damp under my raincoat, like maybe water had been running down the back of my neck. The cold just kept creeping down my spine, and seeping into my fingers and toes, then up my arms and legs.

I'd come a long way since the accident. Fish Camp. Deer Camp. Silver Camp. All the distance I'd covered. I saw it all in my head, like a movie. I had to be close to the Sentinels.

I didn't want to die now. Frozen between two rocks in a rainstorm.

"Noooo!" I screamed. "Not after all this!"

I chewed and swallowed a piece of smoked salmon.

My upper and lower teeth knocked together. My hands and feet numbed as my brain directed more blood to my core. Just like Mr. Haskins said: Your blood retreats to keep your organs working. You can live without your fingers, but try living without your stomach, or your liver or your lungs.

I added more sticks to the fire. Sticks I grabbed between my wrists because my fingers were limp, useless pieces of meat.

When I tried to squat over the fire my legs wouldn't budge, so I just kept leaning against the big rock, and that chilled me even more. You'd think the fire would heat up the rock some, but the fire was small and my body prevented most of the heat from even reaching the rock. If only I could've built a huge fire between the two rocks and let it rage for a few hours, then it would've been like stepping into a heated room, like a sauna. Instead I was trapped in a refrigerator and trying to draw warmth from a candle.

Don't die.

Don't die.

Don't die.

Not here. Not now. I still had my whole life in front of me. Even if I never made it off this island.

I'd build a killer shelter and look for food everywhere, and I'd learn how to use the flint. And if someone came, fine then, but I wanted to live either way.

Sometimes you do all you can do and you still die. I'd fight till the end.

Just like that deer in the hole, it never gave up. It kicked and kicked and even with two broken legs was trying to get out of that hole. Trying to stay alive.

Sometimes you do everything right and you still get hammered.

I turned my head and coughed smoke. Hammered? My dad, he'd want me to live, to survive. If I just gave up, that'd be exactly what he wouldn't have wanted.

And what about my mom? No way would she have given up.

If my mom were still alive, everything would've been different. Our trip would've been different.

But it wasn't different. Mom *had* gone on the bike ride that took her onto the highway and Dad *had* decided to paddle the exposed side of Bear Island. And they'd both taken all kinds of risks in their lives. But how were you supposed to live, anyway? All cautious, never doing anything because you were scared of some unlikely disaster? What kind of life would that be? What they did and why they did it was part of who they were. And what I did, like deciding to not go on that bike ride—that was part of who I was.

Sometime toward morning the heavy rain and wind died, replaced by a fine mist, like the ground had taken as much moisture as it could and was spewing it back as fog.

I jumped up and down, slapped my hands together and rubbed them, slapped my thighs and jumped some more. When my fingers started working, I shoveled salmon into my mouth, then set off southward in the gray of dawn. Slippery rocks made for slow going, but I knew I had to keep moving. Knew, at this moment, that movement was the key to my survival.

I knew I had to make it to the southern end of the island if I was to have any chance of meeting up with other people.

But also, the Sentinels wouldn't be a bad place to die, if it came to that.

At least there I'd be more likely to be found. I could scratch a note into a piece of driftwood, or carve something into a tree so people would know, even if I didn't make it, who I was and that I was a survivor, too. They wouldn't know all that I'd done, but at least they'd know something. That I'd tried my hardest. I could scratch in how many days I'd been out here. Fifty-one so far, if I'd counted right. And I could carve pictures of the deer, porcupine and salmon. The shelters I'd built. And the kayak. The accident. My dad. His voice. The footprints. The life vest. His raincoat. I could tell the whole story in pictures.

The next headland jutted out. I turned inland and clawed my way up the steep, forested land one step at a time. The feeling was coming back in my feet. And I could feel a little sweat on my back from the climb. I topped the spine of the narrow ridge, and looked down on a thumb-shaped bay.

A tingle traveled up my spine and over the top of my head. My breath caught in my throat. One day after the Sentinels we'd paddled around this little bay and then continued north. Close, close, close, I thought, as I studied the drop, seeking an easy way down.

I was so absorbed in my searching that I almost didn't turn around in time. But some way, somehow, a part of me had known—and I turned. And I caught movement, just down the hill, coming my way.

Black, furry movement.

I yelled, "Hey bear," but it kept coming, nose to the ground, not hurrying, but moving steadily. Meandering, as if following my scent. Hunting me.

I looked for a way to get out of the bear's path, for a place I might sit, stand, or crouch so the bear might not notice me, or if it did detect my presence, might not be able to get at me. My eyes turned up nothing at first. Then, far down the hill I spotted some rocks, big rocks. If I could just get to those rocks before the bear got to me.

CHAPTER 33

I UNTIED my raincoat fanny pack, took about half my dried fish and scattered it.

Everyone says, never feed a bear. You'll create a problem. Well, I already had a problem. I ran toward the big rocks, my bowl in one hand, my spear in the other. The hookless gaff I left behind.

Three pillars of black rock, mostly bare, poked out of the ground about two-thirds of the way down the slope. I climbed over a couple fallen trees and kept running, glad that I was going downhill.

I plowed through a patch of leafless blueberry bushes, then dodged some old devil's club stems. I hit another patch of berry bushes. I was high-stepping, twisting my body, just trying to get to those rocks, which were still at least a couple hundred feet below me, when one of my boot-tips caught a root.

I tried to regain my balance, but my other foot got hung up on something and I stumbled, took a few big crazy steps, but then I was falling forward. I tossed the spear sideways before I hit the ground but landed on the backside of the bowl. The bottom of my rib cage on the right side slammed into the bowl at its high point. My side burned like it'd been doused with jet fuel and touched with a match.

I pushed myself up, grabbed the bowl and spear, and kept going, but every breath sent stabbing pains into my side.

I hit the clearing with the rocks and veered left, hoping the bear was still busy. The raincoat that I carried the fish in had loosened up some and was sagging in the back but it was still around my waist.

The top of the middle pillar towered about ten feet off the ground. I dropped my bowl, stuffed a few rocks in my pocket, grabbed onto some brush and climbed up there.

If I could climb this, then so could the bear, but at least I'd be above it if it tried. I stood on top of the pillar and looked upslope. I took tiny breaths to lessen the pain in my side, but even those jabbed me.

I watched as the bear finished the salmon. It kept licking the ground and sniffing around. I was hoping it'd just go back the way it'd come, but then it headed toward me and the pillars.

I crouched down, trying to make myself as small as possible, to become part of the rock. As it came closer I could see that it was a skinny, ragged bear. I didn't know what I'd do if the bear stopped at the pillars, but was hoping for an idea when the time came to act.

Noise hadn't worked with this bear if it was the same one that threatened me at Silver Camp. Banging on a bowl and shouting had brought it closer. And back on the ridge-top it hadn't even looked up when I'd shouted.

Rocks had helped. I wished I had more. And, I really wished I had a big fire between me and the bear. But I didn't.

I couldn't die now. Not by the claws and jaws of some old, deaf bear that probably wouldn't even last the winter. Not after surviving this long and being this close to the Sentinels.

Every nerve ending in my body was on red-alert survival mode sending messages to my brain. Instinct told me to run or hide or fight. And the reasoning part of my brain took this information in and sat with it, waiting to act until the time was right.

Alert but calm, I thought. Alert but calm.

The bear advanced, almost leisurely, seeming intent on following the scent trail. It stopped and sniffed around where I had fallen. Twice more, I saw it stop, rise up and sniff the air. But in the end, it kept coming.

Be the rock, I thought. Just be the rock. I was still crouched and my knees were starting to ache but I didn't want to move, couldn't move, not now. And my side throbbed with every tiny breath. I felt a tug at the back the raincoat carrying the fish and heard little plopping noises and my heart sank. I knew what had just happened. The fish. My fish. I'm not sure how much of it—maybe all of it—had just tumbled down the rocks onto the ground below. I didn't want to turn my head to look because movement was the last thing I wanted the bear to sense.

At the base of the pillars the bear paused, flared its nostrils, then sniffed the ground, and circled the rock formation. Behind me I could hear licking and chewing as it devoured the fish that had fallen from my raincoat. It circled around and stopped just shy of the base of the middle pillar. It pawed at my bowl, then let out a low growl as it sniffed the air again. Twice, the bear slunk away from the pillars and circled back.

All the while I crouched, motionless.

Don't come up here. Don't. I willed my thoughts onto the bear. You stay down there. I'll stay up here. Just leave.

Leave.

Leave.

Leave.

The bear turned away from the pillars and I rose, a rock in one hand, my spear in the other, and stood absolutely still, like a statue. An extension of the rock. I could feel the raincoat hanging free. It was empty. Completely empty.

The bear shuffled back as before but seemed more agitated, like maybe it sensed a change. I wished I hadn't moved, but I needed to be ready.

It approached the middle pillar, and then backed off, uttering a low growl. And I just stood there. I knew if I did anything now, the fight was on. And I didn't want to fight a bear. Especially an old bear that wasn't hibernating. A desperate bear who might do desperate things.

It advanced again, remaining on all four legs and lifting its head as it came forward all the way to the middle pillar. The bear started to rise up on its hind legs.

I cocked my arm and let the fist-sized stone fly, pain searing my side. A dead-center shot to the snout. The bear growled, then stood all the way up and kept coming, its big paws and jaws closing the distance.

I thrust my spear, jabbing the bear in the eye and twisting with both arms as hard as I could. The bear made some kind of horrible screaming sound and pulled back. I held on to the spear with the bear twisting its head and shaking it. I was losing my footing, being drawn off the rock, and my side was exploding with pain like there was a demon hatching out of it.

Then the spear popped free—without the hook. The momentum pitched me backwards and my feet caught only air. I reached my arms forward, still gripping the spear and it caught the top of the pillar and I pulled myself back up, then stood. Below me, threads of fishing line dangled from the bear's bloody eye socket. I threw another rock, hammering the bear in the nose. My third throw missed the bear's hind end by inches as it started to retreat.

My heart beat in my throat and roared in my ears. I was wet—wet with sweat from head to toe.

I sat on the pillar, my legs hanging over the edge, and watched the bear disappear over the ridge. Energy drained from me like water rushing down a river. I bowed my head, and pulled air into my lungs in short breaths. I covered my face with my hands.

I sat and breathed—nothing else. I wished I could breathe my way home. I closed my eyes. Images of my mom, then my dad, flashed in my mind. Then I saw the salmon, the deer, the berries, the otters, the shelters I'd built. I felt the rise and fall of my chest, the steady burn in my side, and the warm air pushing past my hands after it left my nose.

After a while, I started to shiver from lack of movement. All that sweat had cooled off.

I'd need a fire soon. Maybe I'd just build one at the base of this rock; that way if the bear came back I could scramble up here again.

I raised my head, and glanced at the end of the hookless spear darkened by the bear's blood.

I was alive, living.

No matter what happens, I thought, no matter what, even if the bear comes back, everything will be okay.

THE ACCIDENT

When I surfaced, I spit water and sucked air. Pieces of red fiberglass bobbed in the water. I searched for the orange of my dad's life vest but didn't see it. Maybe he was just out of sight in the trough of a nearby wave, or maybe he'd started for shore. Then another wave pushed me under.

CHAPTER 34

THE NEXT day I hiked through the low notch at the back of the thumb-shaped bay and then through the muskeg above the Sentinels.

Now, as I stood on the gravel beach, so finely ground that it was almost sand in places, with the big trees behind me, I let out a sigh. The water was glassy. I wished it was being carved up by a boat.

Yeah, I'd made it this far, but thanks to the bear I had no fish and no more hooks. And my right side ached whenever I bent or twisted or reached, or if I took a deep breath. An ugly purple bruise the size and shape of a hotdog had popped up on my ribs right where I'd fallen on the bowl. And my lighter had sparked its last fire last night.

I turned from the protected cove, crossed the most recent strand line, and walked into the trees. Smooth beach gravel covered the spit that housed the Sentinels—flat ground with little brush under a canopy of enormous trees. Trees my mom loved. Trees my dad loved.

I looked toward the sky. And I waved.

Yeah, waved.

Just in case Mom could see me. And Dad, well, he wasn't here.

I walked to the spot where Dad and I had pitched our tent. Then the other spot where our kitchen tarp had been.

Back then I hadn't thought much about our possessions. The tent, the sleeping pads, the sleeping bags, the small cook-stove, the tarps, the store-bought food. There it was, food, again entering my mind.

Without food this drop-dead beautiful place was a place to drop dead. A lonely place to die where birds and bears and bugs would pick me apart. It didn't really matter how much my parents loved this place or what they'd done here. What mattered was now. Right now.

I tried to grasp the feeling of peace I'd experienced yesterday after I'd fought the bear, the feeling that no matter what happened everything would be okay, but it kept slipping from my mind.

And I thought, maybe this is how it is. That sometimes you can feel like everything will be okay but you can't feel like that all the time. And if you can just remember that you once felt that way, if you can just keep the idea alive, then maybe the feeling will come back again. Kind of like keeping a fire going just enough so there are always coals to restart it.

I put my stuff at the base of the biggest Sentinel, planning to make my shelter there. I was really hoping I wouldn't have to build another shelter. That I'd see my dad, or if not him, then meet some people and they'd take me back so I could start my new life as an orphan. It'd be easy to die here. But I didn't want easy. I wanted life.

Scattered high clouds were invading the blue sky. A slight breeze blew from the south.

I noticed a dark spot just above the strand line and walked over to it. I reached down and ran my hand across the rocks and it came back coated with gray.

Ash.

Ash from a fire. My heart did a little dance.

There were older strand lines above the ash-covered rocks so this spot would eventually get wiped clean. I saw some little dents in the gravel. Footprints that would be erased by a higher tide. I stared at the fire-darkened patch of gravel, like it had a secret to tell me.

"Whoever made this, who are you? Where are you? When will you be back?"

The tides, what did I know about the tides? They cycled with the moon, like a monthly cycle. So, at certain parts of the cycle the tide would come in higher than during other parts of the cycle. So, probably this fire was made within the last month. Maybe two days ago. Maybe two weeks ago. And it'd probably be gone after this cycle's highest tide.

But someone had been here. And twisted up, just above the strand line behind the fire was something gray. I walked a few steps, crouched down and scooped up a thin piece of cloth. An old-looking gray, salt-hardened bandana.

My heart pounded in my head.

My dad's face invaded my brain. He always carried a bandana, used it as a handkerchief. And he had a bunch of different colored ones. I pictured him sitting here. I cradled the bandana in both hands.

"Dad. Is this yours?" I held the bandana up to the sky. "Is it?" I shouted.

I waited for his voice, but was met with silence.

It could be anyone's. But, it could be his.

I pictured a boat coming and rescuing him. And him being so excited that he forgot he'd left his bandana on the beach.

But then wouldn't he be searching the coast for me? I'd spent most of my time at the back of Hidden Bay and then tucked into Deer Camp and Silver Camp. And I'd had to walk inland many times to avoid cliffs, so a searching boat could've missed me easily. But they would've seen the yellow spray skirt I'd tied to the top of the stick. And surely they'd come back here. And they'd see the word 'Sentinels' I'd left in rocks at Fish Camp and Silver Camp. I was so depressed when I left Deer Camp that I didn't leave a sign.

I started to cool down from lack of movement, so I stuffed the bandana into my pocket and walked through the trees to a trickle of a stream I remembered using as a water source.

I rinsed the bandana with fresh water and rung it out. Then I filled my bowl and was making my way back to my gear when I saw the junk pile bumping up from the forest floor.

Used to be a sauna, I remembered.

I set the bowl down and walked over to the pile. Images of me and Dad standing on this site filled my brain. I shook my head, tried to clear my thoughts. I needed to focus on the present if I wanted any chance of having a future.

I grabbed a moss-covered board and tossed it aside. I grabbed another one and it broke apart in my hands. So I just started grabbing the spongy boards one at a time, and if they didn't break apart, I set them aside. At first a knife stabbed my side every time I reached or pulled, but over time it turned into an ache that was just there, like the knife was just stuck in me for good.

I salvaged eleven two-by-fours, each about eight feet long. I hauled these to the biggest Sentinel, and then went back to the pile.

What was left was so rotten I couldn't even tell where one board started and another ended. Using my feet, I pushed the wood mush aside. Then my boot slid on something firm.

I stooped down, pushed the rest of the mush away with my hands and saw ridged metal.

"The roof," I said, "Part of the roof of the sauna."

The junk pile also turned up half a dozen plastic five-gallon buckets, but the metal roofing, a single four-by-eight-foot sheet peppered with holes, was by far the most valuable item.

I leaned two ten-foot-long deadfall poles against the big tree starting about six feet up the trunk, spaced about three feet apart.

I used the last of my rope to lash a two-by-four to the poles four feet down from the big tree. Then I put the metal roofing between the two-by-four and the tree and used the rest of the two-by-fours to complete the roof.

I covered the roof and floor with spruce boughs, lined the base of the shelter opposite the tree with rocks and built fire rings on both ends of the shelter, which was about eight feet long and six feet tall at its tallest point against the tree.

I could almost hear LF and RF starting to nag me. But the truth was, if I couldn't get the flint to work, they wouldn't exist. On the far sides of the fire rings I stacked piles of boughs waist high in semicircles and weighted them with rocks, hoping to keep the wind out.

Dad would love my shelter. Love that I'd taken that pile of junk and turned it into something useful.

But hunger gnawed at me, and lack of energy slowed my work.

I pulled the flint from my pocket. Sparks. Sparks. Sparks. I knew it'd shoot sparks but I had to have the right material to transform those sparks into a fire. I wished the lighter still worked. If I could get one more flame from it that's all I'd need, but I'd tried and tried—that puppy was dead.

I looked up at the hemlock trees, focusing on branches that didn't have any needles. I knew the tiny ends of those branches worked great when dry and touched to a flame but how could I get them to do their thing with just sparks? I ripped some dead branches from the trees and made a knee-high pile in front of my shelter. I broke the spindly ends off the branches and rubbed the tiny twigs between my hands. Little bits of brown and off-white wood particles sprinkled onto my dad's old raincoat, which I'd spread below me for that very reason. I kept pulverizing the tiny twigs until I'd used them all. Then I took a branch about as big around as a paper-towel core and started shaving it, letting my blade barely touch it. I wanted shavings so thin that they'd crumble when I picked them up.

"Thin. Thin. Thin. Thin."

Back at the wall tent I always thought things were so primitive, so basic. But not anymore. I mean, things were simple out there, but anything we wanted, we could just bring it from the house. Need some really dry fire-starting material? Just let it sit behind the wood stove for a few days, that'd suck the moisture out of it, or grab some dryer lint. They didn't call it a dryer for nothing. It dried things. And dry things caught fire a lot easier than damp things, especially if you're starting a fire from a spark.

Curly shavings were piling up on the raincoat and mixing in with the pulverized bits from the twigs, all in the fading daylight. I scooped the shavings and wood bits up with two hands and packed them together like I was making a snowball. I set the ball down into the center of what I hoped would become RF. It sprung outward when I released my hands but still held its shape. I molded the mess back together, then stuck my finger straight down into it, making a little depression. This looked as close to a nest of dryer lint as I'd ever gotten.

I stood up and stretched my arms over my head and took a deep breath. And I was struck again by the fact that I was here—that I'd made it here on my own. I felt a shiver go up my spine, and then tingles at the back of my nose. Would anyone come? And, would they come in time?

I knelt in front of the wood shavings, and positioned the flint so the tip rested in the depression I'd made.

See the fire. Just see it happen. Believe it will happen.

I closed my eyes and saw sparks, hundreds of sparks. Thousands. Like fireworks. Exploding from the flint. Raining everywhere. Starting fires everywhere. I heard the flames crackling and spitting.

I opened my eyes and ran the knife up and down on the flint. At first a couple sparks fell and died in the wood-shaving nest. Then I got the angle right and I was getting a shower of sparks with every swipe of the blade. The nest started to part in the middle as the flint pressed into it, but I kept running the knife faster and faster.

A thin wisp of smoke rose from the side of the nest and I dropped the flint leaned forward and blew gently. A red glow answered, followed by more smoke, then nothing.

My shoulders collapsed forward. All those sparks for one tiny wisp of smoke that didn't even turn into a fire. I cupped the shavings and wood particles in my hands, squeezed them into a ball, set them down and rained more sparks onto them.

Come on, I thought. Just this one time. All I need is one flame. I closed my eyes and just kept running the knife up and down the flint. In my mind I saw sparks, or maybe I was seeing images of the real things through my eyelids. Part of me didn't believe the flint would work, and part of me felt like I was failure because I had this fire-starting tool and couldn't get it to work. And all the time I just kept running the knife on the flint, keeping my eyes closed. I could feel the wood shavings brushing my knuckles as my hand moved.

"Fire, fire, fire," I started singing.

> Light of life in my soul
> Warm me with flame
> Make me whole

Lyrics from one of my mom's unfinished songs scribbled in a notebook she'd kept in her guitar case. I kept singing the lines over and over even though I wasn't sure what they meant.

My arms grew warm from the movement while my feet were turning to ice. I kept running the knife and concentrating on the lyrics. I sucked air through my nose, and my eyes flew open. Three streams of smoke were rising from the wood-shaving nest. I sat back on my heels, pivoted on my hips so my face was almost in the smoking nest and gently blew. Several red eyes stared back at me and one of them burned brighter than the rest, and then burst into a thin flame.

That night I dreamed of the accident, and this time I saw it, the whole thing. My dad bobbing in front of the rock reef and then the big wave, the wave that pushed me under, smashing him against the rocks, and then him floating—facedown. I saw it happen three times. Saw his life vest hanging off his bare arm because he wasn't wearing his raincoat. I saw it all.

In the morning I stoked RF and LF and then leaned against the Sentinel. My mind was a mess of thoughts. Was the dream telling me what had really happened? Was that my dad communicating to me? Or had I known it all along? Did I see that happen for real during the accident? I mean, it seemed so real in the dream. But the bandana I'd found. I'd dried it out last night and then tied it around my neck as an added layer for warmth. And the raincoat? Was it really his?

"Whatever happened, happened," RF said.

"What's happening now is what matters," LF said.

"Just shut up so I can think." I ran my hand across the bandana. "This could be his."

"If you're gonna think," RF said, crackling. "Think about something helpful. Not something that'll drag you down."

"You said it yourself," LF said. "No matter what happens, everything will be okay."

"Yeah, but that was before the dream," I said. "If only I'd seen that rock sooner. If I hadn't closed my eyes..."

"You're not telling yourself anything new, big boy," RF said. "You're just finally accepting it."

"Sometimes your mind won't let you see things for a while," LF said, "because it's not good for you. And then when the time is right, the information seems new, but really it's always been there. You never discover anything that didn't already exist."

"But if I'd known," I said, "then I would've eaten these the minute I found them." I laid the Meal Pack bars down in front of LF. My whole body was shaking, trembling. I touched the bandana again. I lay on my back and rested my head on my dad's life vest. I took the shredded raincoat in my hands, brought it to my lips, and then hugged it to my chest. In my mind it'd always be his even if I didn't know for sure anymore. What were the chances I'd find a raincoat that looked just like his? I reached out one hand, grabbed the Meal Pack bars and laid them on top of my stomach and let my breaths raise and lower them. And I listened.

Eat them now. It's okay. Everything is okay. Everything you did was okay. Everything.

CHAPTER 35

THE MEAL

Pack bars I'd saved forever lessened my hunger for a couple of hours and then I was right back where I'd left off—starving. My stomach was like an eroded riverbank with my rib cage hanging over the top. And then when I'd drink a few bowlfuls of warm water, my stomach would bulge like I'd swallowed a big round rock. And the dream kept popping into my mind. Was it just a dream or was it really what had happened? And my dad's voice saying: Everything I did was okay.

I touched the bandana covering my neck and said, "Everything you did was okay too, Dad. Everything."

In the cold rain I walked to the shore and scanned the horizon. No boat. No boat. No boat. It was low tide and the mussel beds stretched out in front of me.

What did Dad say? Eating shellfish is risky. They could be good one day and bad the next. You never know if they're going to be toxic. You could die.

I thought about all I'd been through. The mistakes I'd made and the consequences I'd lived with. What I had to lose. What I had to gain. And then I knew what I had to do.

I pulled the mussels from the cold mud and threw them into a bucket. They came away in groups, still attached to the rocks anchoring them. Small, black, and hard, each one closed tight. I kept tossing them in until the bottom of the bucket was covered, then headed to my shelter.

I warmed my numb hands by LF, then cut the mussels from their anchors and plopped half a dozen of them into the bowl, which was filled with water and just coming to a gentle boil on RF. I decided to start with a few mussels on the outside chance that if they were poisonous, then eating just a few might only make me sick and not kill me.

I let them roll in the boiling water until I could see the shells separating, then herded the mussels to the side of the bowl with a piece of driftwood. With my fingers I fished them onto the lid of a five-gallon bucket.

In the firelight I could see steam drifting from the hot shells. At least I had a warm shelter. The windbreaks, plus the killer roof, kept it pretty warm as long as I had wood to keep RF and LF going.

But without food, it was just a warm place to die.

If only I could've killed that bear. All that meat. Maybe it was dead, but I'd never know. And I hadn't tried to kill it. I was just trying to keep from getting killed. Maybe I should've driven the spear farther instead of pulling it out. Or stabbed it again instead of throwing that second rock. Maybe that was the difference—I had to think like a predator, instead of prey.

As for the mussels, I think I'd rather fight the bear again than eat them. The closer you are to death, the more chances you take, that's what I thought. If Dad were here, and was a shriveled up wreck like me, he might make the same choice.

I lifted a mussel off the lid and pried it the rest of the way open with my thumbs. In one of the half shells lay a small hunk of gray tissue.

"Sure you want to do that?" RF asked.

I nodded.

"There's no going back, once you do," LF said.

"Back to where?" I said. "Back to starving?"

"Forget it," LF said. "Just eat."

I scooped the mussel partway out of the shell with my index finger, then grabbed it with my front teeth and pulled. It was chewy and had a strong, fishy taste.

After consuming the six mussels, I stoked the fires, lay down on top of the life vests, and covered myself with the emergency blankets, hoping to be alive come morning.

CHAPTER 36

HOURS LATER, I woke.

The mussels.

My stomach, it felt okay. I pulled air through my nose, and smiled.

I placed small sticks on top of RF's coals and blew until I saw smoke, then flames. I built up the fire and let it burn down. Then from the bucket I added more mussels to the bowl and put it on the coals.

I pulled my boots on and stepped outside. A cold, wet wind was blowing snow sideways. I jogged to the shore to take care of business and a small flash of light caught my eyes and disappeared. I squinted and tried to see through the blowing snow across the water. It flashed again.

"Hello!" I yelled. "Hello! I'm over here!"

And I kept on yelling, and every yell stabbed my side. And I kept looking, squinting. Now I could hear the deep hum of a motor. I saw the flash again, then again. It was moving away from the cove toward the point closest to the mainland. Of course, it was gonna cross at the point, the same way Dad and I crossed to get to Bear Island.

I kept screaming and waving through the snow, and jumping up and down, hoping that whoever it was would hear me or see me and turn.

I looked for that flash to grow closer, but the next flash I saw was farther away. I kept looking and looking. And yelling. And the hum of the motor faded in and out. After a while I didn't hear it anymore. I yelled and yelled and kept scanning the water but saw nothing. Probably motoring across to the mainland by now.

I fell to my knees and they sunk into the wet gravel. Then I lay on my side, facing the water. I felt a few snowflakes land on my cheek. Just cover me up, I thought. Cover me up and get it over with.

So close, I was so close. But close didn't matter if I didn't make it off the island. I was still here. I wasn't any closer to anything. Nothing had changed. And I felt farther away than I ever had.

Farther than when I'd found my dad's vest and not him.

Farther than when I'd learned that my mom had died in a hit and run accident.

Farther than after I'd had that dream about my dad.

The wake from the boat started washing onto the shore. A wave touched my feet and I pushed myself up from the beach and headed back to my shelter.

I had to live like I was never gonna get rescued because if I didn't live like this, then there was no way I'd gather enough food and firewood to keep me going. I couldn't rely on anyone. Maybe a dozen boats would pass by off shore like that one.

I fished the mussels from the bowl and ate them. There had to be thirty or forty of them, but they were small and I was still hungry so I took a bucket and got more mussels, boiled them up and ate them. I'd just eat mussels every day and gather a ton of firewood. And wait. I'd wait forever if I had to. I'd wait for the rest of my life.

———

I made the long hike to the point, up and down over spiky headlands. I wanted to leave some kind of marker, something that would show someone coming from the mainland that something wasn't right. But I didn't want to part with my life vests or emergency blankets. I thought about tying my dad's raincoat to a tree, but it was blue, which isn't the brightest color to attract attention.

I would've camped on the point if I could, but it was too exposed.

So I brought two yellow five-gallon buckets with me. At the point I filled them with rocks and set them up high. They didn't point exactly to where I was, but it was the best I could do.

On the hike back my stomach cramped up. Maybe my body couldn't take the mussels in large quantities like it did the salmon. I wasn't keeling over and vomiting blood, but cramps and diarrhea kept hammering me.

There were lots of mussels, but if I couldn't keep them inside my body, then it didn't matter.

Still, I hoped small amounts of them would be enough, just enough for me to hang on if I didn't find something else to eat. And maybe my stomach would get used to them.

———

Two days later, snow continued to blow without sticking as darkness fell. The tide was high, covering the mussel beds, and I was collecting firewood. I never felt like I had enough wood.

I knew a big storm could blow in and confine me to my shelter for several days, so I wanted a cushion of wood, but the more I collected the farther I had to go to get it. And the more energy I put into collecting wood, the more food I needed to fuel my body. And I could only eat so many mussels at a time before stomach problems set in.

But I knew I needed more food. My clothing hung limp on my body. Sometimes I'd feel a little energy surge after eating some mussels, but not for very long.

What choice did I have? Not having enough wood meant the same as not having enough food.

———

A week passed and still no one came. The high tides had come and erased the fire-darkened patch of rocks where I'd found the bandana. Sixty-five scratches on my spear. And the snow had stuck. The Sentinels kept a lot of it off the spit, but when I went in search of firewood I was plowing through six inches of wet snow.

I kept eating the mussels, and they still gave me stomach problems. And having diarrhea in the snow was no joke, especially trudging down to the shore in the dark with my insides twisting and screaming.

I found a few shriveled berries, but they did little to combat my deep hunger. I looked for animals, hoped for another porcupine, but didn't see any. Just a few bird tracks in the snow. Still, I pushed myself forward, my mind telling my body to keep going. If I could just hang on until I found something to eat or until someone came. Just keep living, I told myself, even if only barely, because you never know when you'll get a break, when you'll get lucky. But if you're dead, there's no way to get lucky.

I was gathering firewood on a slope and slipped. I tried to regain my balance, but I must've tripped on a rock or a root beneath the snow because all of a sudden I was in the air going sideways and then I landed on my ankle. Pain burned into my foot and partway up my shin. And my whole lower leg and foot kept on burning and buzzing like it was going numb, except it hurt at the same time.

I limped back to camp with a little wood. My ankle swelled up and pressed into my rubber boot, and pain shot through my lower leg when I put weight on it.

I tried to rest it for a day, but if I wasn't moving around I needed more wood to stay warm, and if I needed more wood to stay warm I needed to get more wood, which was hard to do with an ankle you couldn't put weight on.

I dragged my leg through the snow and got what wood I could. My wood supply dwindled. I ate more mussels, but knew they weren't enough.

I tried to will that feeling back—that feeling that everything would be okay—but the harder I tried the farther away it went.

———

I scratched my eightieth line onto my spear, and lay back down. It was morning, time to gather some mussels, but I just lay there. I closed my eyes and felt the air going in and out of my lungs in shallow breaths. I tried to breathe deeper but couldn't.

I felt warm even though RF and LF had burned down to coals and weren't putting off much heat. Wood, I thought. I needed to put some wood on them. I'd managed to keep a fire going ever since I'd been here and didn't want to have to face using the flint again.

"In a minute. In a minute. In a minute," I whispered.

A ringing sound invaded my ears. It just kept coming and going. Fading in and out. Like someone was humming a tune. Like the way my mom used to hum while she drew. And then I saw her, at the kitchen table, humming and drawing. And throwing a smile my way.

I drifted off with the humming, with my mom, and that feeling came back—that everything would be okay, no matter what happened.

A scraping noise forced its way in to my awareness, blotting my mom out. I opened my eyes and saw the metal roofing and remembered where I was. I put my hands over my face. They smelled fishy, like mussels. Then I remembered that I needed to drag my leg down to the shore to get some mussels.

I closed my eyes again, and felt warm.

Warm all over.

And saw my mom, and my dad. They were smiling at each other, holding hands, standing under a big tree, one of the Sentinels. I walked toward them, and they held their arms out.

I heard gulls squawking. Something I hadn't heard in days. Really since Silver Camp. I lifted my chin and rolled onto my side. A cold rush of air nudged me, and I coughed. RF and LF, I couldn't let them go all the way out. But I just lay there. Closed my eyes and there they were—Mom and Dad. We were at home on the deck, eating hand-cranked, homemade ice cream.

But the gull squawks slammed my ears again. Like they were right outside my shelter. They were coming for me, for my eyes. I sucked in a few short breaths.

No, I thought. No. I'm not ready to die. Not ready to lose my eyes.

But they kept squawking.

I stretched my arms over my head and opened my eyes. I'd show them. Show them that I was alive. That I could fight them, and win. Kill one and eat it. I dragged myself forward with my elbows, grabbed my spear, and stuck my head out of the shelter. Through the blowing snow I saw no gulls but kept hearing their taunts over and over.

I squinted, and my heart jumped into my throat.

Two green blurs were marching toward me.

I opened my eyes wide.

Two people, real people, clad in green raingear were moving toward me, walking just above the highest strand line, shouting *hellooo* over and over.

I tried to talk, formed the word *help* in my brain, but all that came out of my mouth was a muffled grunt.

One of them lifted a hand and waved.

I raised my spear, then let it fall.

My eyes closed and I saw Mom and Dad again. Just their faces—smiling against a sky of puffy white clouds. Their faces kept getting smaller and smaller until they disappeared and my mind was a wall of clouds.

But the crunching sound of boots on snow and gravel filled my ears along with more shouts of *helloooo*. I forced my eyes open again, and felt them grow hot with tears.

I didn't know where I was going, or who I'd be living with, but I was getting off this island.

I was going to live.

THE END

NOTES FROM THE AUTHOR

PRINCE WILLIAM SOUND is a real place on the Alaskan Coastline. Over the past twenty-four years I have paddled a sea kayak many hundreds of miles in the Sound, exploring the remote, jagged coastline and camping on uninhabited islands alone and with friends. The first time I went sea kayaking was in 1991 and it turned into a nine week, five-hundred-mile adventure. I was hooked!

I have written many journals about my experiences in Prince William Sound. On one solo kayaking trip, I cooked salmon the way Tom cooks them. I have watched bears fish for salmon, have taken a fall on a mountain similar to the one Tom takes, and have paddled through big seas and breaking waves.

Fortunately, I was never stranded, but a couple of times when I was in rough waters, I felt I was a few paddle strokes from disaster.

While Bear Island is a fictional island, the places Tom discovers on his journey on Bear Island are based on and inspired by places I have a spent time exploring while on wilderness sea kayak trips in Prince William Sound.

ACKNOWLEDGMENTS Many thanks to all my friends who've spent time with me on wilderness trips over the past thirty years. All of those experiences have played into the creation of this story. Thanks to my early readers Lisa Muscavage, Natalie Bahm, Robert Guthrie, Eva Saulitis, Lou Brown, Carol Lynch Williams, Terry Lynn Johnson and Carl Greci. A big thank you to my agent, Amy Tipton, who not only found a home for my story but also was instrumental in the final rewrites before putting it on submission. Thanks to Eileen Robinson and all the great people at Move Books who worked hard to make this the best book it could be. And finally, a thank you to my wife, Dana, for believing in me as writer, letting me use some of her song lyrics in the story, and for reading countless drafts and offering her expertise as a writer.